"Can you forgiv
I hadn't come?"

Brent offered a half smile, and her arm warmed and tingled under his hand. "Of course I forgive you. You're doing your best and you've been very brave."

"Thank you," she squeaked. It was all she could manage.

He turned his head to look at the sun high over her shoulder. "If you really don't feel you belong here, I won't keep you here against your will. I'll take you back to the train station the day after tomorrow if that's what you want."

Christy looked down at his hand, still resting on her arm. His touch was softer than she'd imagined it would be. *But if this isn't where I belong, even his touch making me feel alive inside for the first time in a long time can't change that. Was I only fooling myself to think that this scheme could ever work out?*

She pulled her arm from his grasp. "We'd best find your horse and wagon, then." For the other concern, she didn't have a solution.

Vivi Holt lives in beautiful Brisbane, Australia, with her husband, three children and their three guinea pigs. After a career as a knowledge manager, she is now living her dream of writing full-time. When she's not writing, she loves to hike, read, sing and travel. As a former student of history, Vivi especially enjoys creating unique and thrilling tales inspired by true historical events.

The UNEXPECTED MARRIAGE BARGAIN

VIVI HOLT

Previously published as *Christy* & *Ramona*

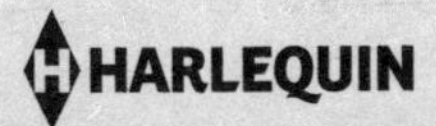

Recycling programs for this product may not exist in your area.

ISBN-13: 978-1-335-95797-9

The Unexpected Marriage Bargain

This edition published by arrangement with Harlequin Books S.A.

For questions and comments about the quality of this book, please contact us at CustomerService@Harlequin.com.

Harlequin Enterprises ULC
22 Adelaide St. West, 40th Floor
Toronto, Ontario M5H 4E3, Canada
www.Harlequin.com

Printed in U.S.A.

CONTENTS

CHRISTY

Prologue

July 29, 1886

The horse galloped across the open field, eyes wide and nostrils flared. Brent Taylor could see Annabelle's face pale as she clung to the palomino's back, the reins bunched tightly in her whitened fist. A clap of thunder filled the humid Kentucky air, and the horse lifted its head with a shake and sped up.

"Anna, hold on!" he yelled, but the wind seemed to catch it and throw it back in his face. He wasn't sure she could hear him at all. He rushed to the horse yard by the barn, caught a bridle hanging on the gate post and quickly pushed it over the ears of the bay standing idle there. The gate bounced open with a flick of his wrist and he jumped onto the horse, leaned over its arched neck and tapped its ribs with his heels. "Let's go, Patty."

The beast leaped forward and through the gate, desperately following Annabelle.

The palomino mare was her favorite horse, but had always been flighty and unpredictable. Brent had never liked her riding it. But she'd insisted, saying her mane was perfect for braiding and her dainty head was so pretty, she just couldn't bear to give her up. Now it was taking her across the field nearest the house, headed toward the main road. Surely the mare would stop soon?

Brent was following and gradually gaining on her. Her free arm flailed above the horse, and he silently cursed the sidesaddle she insisted on using. "Ladies don't ride astride, darling," she'd said as she flipped her blonde braid over her shoulder and smiled at him.

"No one will ever know but me," he protested. But she'd just tipped her head to one side and looked at him with those big blue eyes, and he'd relented. She could do what she wished, then.

"Hold on. I'm coming!" Brent cried into the wind. His brown Stetson blew from his head, tumbling to land on a tussock of black-eyed susans. Lightning spiked from the sky to the earth, and he braced himself for the crash that followed.

The palomino leaped over a rocky outcropping and stumbled. Brent watched helplessly as Annabelle flew over the horse's lowered shoulder and landed with a thud on the rocks below. "No," he whispered.

He reached Annabelle within moments, jumping from Patty's back to the ground below and running to her. She lay unmoving, her braid loose, waves of straight hair covering her face. He knelt beside her and lifted her head into his lap. "Anna, darling." He smoothed her hair and dipped his ear to her mouth to listen for her breath. Nothing. Her face was pallid and she was limp in his arms. A trickle of blood ran from her left temple and her eyes were closed. She was gone.

He pulled her to his chest, his arms wrapped tightly

around her, and rocked her back and forth. He let the tears fall as fat raindrops hit the dusty ground around them.

"Anna. My darling Anna..."

Chapter One

February 1889

A chill wind blew up and over the woolen muffler around Christy Hancock's neck. She pulled it tighter and lifted the edge of it over her mouth, clutched the folder of piano music to her chest and lowered her head into the wind. If only spring would hurry up and come to Philadelphia.

She loved spring in Philadelphia. It snuck in from the south on a warm breeze, melted away the ice and snow, and enticed flocks of geese, ducks and other seasonal fowl back to the skies in formation, as they made their way north for another summer. She longed for the sweetness of sunshine and the squirrels skipping and frolicking, rather than seeing the shivering creatures settled on bare branches along the frozen boulevard.

She flicked the latch on the gate and headed up the garden path to the front door of her parents' red-brick three-level home. The door wasn't locked, so she slipped inside and slammed it shut behind her, leaning against it in relief as the warmth of the house enveloped her.

She sighed and unwrapped herself from the labyrinth of wool—scarf, muffler, hat, and coat—hanging each piece on the coat rack by the door. "Mam, I'm home!"

There was no response. She stepped into the parlor and set the sheet music in its place on the piano, then made her way into the kitchen, finding it empty as well. A large plate of warm ginger cookies, Christy's favorite, was the only sign anyone was home. She selected one and took a great bite, savoring the sweet and spicy taste of it in her mouth. Dropping another two cookies into the pockets of her skirt, she went around the house in search of her mother.

She finally found her in the sitting room, staring out the front window at the street, a half-finished sweater bundled in her lap, knitting needles poking out of the yarn at odd angles. "There you are, Mam. I've been looking for you." Christy took another bite of cookie, catching the falling crumbs with her free hand.

"Christy, please don't eat in here. How many times have I told you that?"

"Sorry, Mam."

"How were your piano lessons?"

"Fine, thank you. Mrs. Oldsberg says I'm ready for fifth-level examinations. They're to be held in April. What do you think?"

"I'm sure you would do well."

Christy's mother seemed distracted. Generally she would press her to do a piano examination, but this time she barely responded before she resumed staring out the window. "Is something the matter, Mam?" she asked, joining her mother on the horsehair settee.

"No, nothing's wrong, my dear. Only… Daddy and

I do have something to discuss with you." She turned to face Christy with a wan smile.

"Oh? Well, what is it?"

"We should wait until Daddy gets home. I'm expecting him at any moment."

"Oh fiddle-dee-dee, Mam—you know you're going to tell me anyway. So let's have it—what's on your mind? Daddy won't care a jot if you tell me on your own, you know he won't. And anyway, you're starting to scare me." Christy studied her mother's face with concern. What could it be?

Was Daddy ill? No. Christy shook the thought away—it had to be something pleasant. Perhaps they'd decided to get her a horse for Christmas after all. Or maybe they were all going to take that long-deliberated trip to Ireland to see the extended family. She could barely contain her excitement as she thought about the possibilities. She desperately longed to see Europe, and her parents had always been so very unfair on the subject, telling her she was too young to go alone, or that they couldn't afford to go as a family. Maybe they were finally ready!

Mrs. Hancock's face twisted as she thought, and Christy could tell she was close to yielding. She took her mother's hands in hers and smiled. "Come now, Mam. You'll feel better for the telling."

"Oh, all right. Christy Hancock, you are the most difficult child to refuse." Mrs. Hancock grinned despite herself and drew a deep breath. "We're moving."

"What?" Christy's eyes grew wide.

"Daddy has been offered a job in California, and we're going there in just a few weeks. I'm sorry, my dear—I know you love it here, and your friends are here, but your father believes it will be for the best. Do you remember Wesley Combs, Daddy's friend?"

Christy nodded, her eyes filling with unshed tears.

"As you know, he moved to San Francisco five years ago. He opened a lumber yard there, and apparently it has been doing very well. He needs someone to manage it, since he's expanding and can't possibly cope with it all himself, and he wants your father because he doesn't want to entrust it to anyone out there. He's willing to pay four times what your father is making now."

"But Mam, are you saying I have to go too?" Her voice choked over the words.

"Now, now, my dear—only if you wish to. You're nineteen now and capable of making your own decisions. You know we want you to come with us, but we understand if you'd rather stay. We'd have to find a suitable arrangement for you, of course, but it is possible—if that's what you want." Her mother squeezed her hands and smiled at her.

Tears slid down Christy's cheeks. "No, I couldn't stay behind without you and Daddy." She was whispering, but the sentiment was firm. Her heart lay with her family, and her parents were the only family she had. The idea of living in a big city on her own, even a city she loved, was overwhelming. She couldn't bear the thought of it, and she fell with a cry onto Mrs. Hancock's yarn-covered lap.

Mrs. Hancock stroked her hair with a sigh. "Of course you can come with us, my dear. I just didn't want to drag you all the way out to California against your will. It's pioneer territory, my dear, and while Daddy felt we should insist you come with us, I asked him to give you the choice, and he agreed."

"I'm coming with you." Christy sniffled into Mrs. Hancock's skirts.

"All right, my dear."

The front door blew open and an icy wind pushed Mr. Hancock inside with a single gust. He turned to close it quickly, then faced the women across the hall. "I see you've told her," he said.

"Yes."

"And?"

"She's coming with us."

Mr. Hancock wiped a hand across his brow, relief evident on his reddened face. "Well, thank the good Lord for that."

Chapter Two

"You're moving to California?" Candice Sinnamon's eyebrows arched in surprise.

"Yes, I'm afraid so," replied Christy, tracing a finger around the floral print of her skirt, her face glum. The two girls sat in Candice's bedroom—Christy on the edge of the feather bed, Candice in a rocking chair with her feet tucked beneath her petticoats. The walls were covered with pastel-pink wallpaper and a pile of plush toys and dolls decorated the bed, reminders of a childhood not long left behind.

"But I'll never see you again."

"You might, though I suppose it's not particularly likely. My life is ruined." Christy flung herself down on the bed and buried her face in a pillow.

"I don't know, it sounds kind of exciting to me." Candice grimaced. "I never get to go anywhere. My parents won't even let me visit my Aunt Petunia in New York."

"I suppose you could be right." Christy rolled onto her back and sat up, smoothing her unruly red curls against her head with both palms.

"Of course I'm right. You'll get to see all kinds of

thrilling new places and do things that are frowned upon here. I've heard you can even ride astride a horse out West and no one even bats an eye. Not to mention the cowboys you'll meet."

"You think I'll meet cowboys?"

"In California? You're bound to. They're everywhere out there."

"Ooooh." Christy clapped her hands together in glee and her eyes misted over at the thought. Surely all cowboys were handsome, romantic men who sat around in the starlight whistling tunes over restless cattle. They'd be well-mannered and wear big hats and riding boots and say things like "howdy" and "dang." "I hadn't thought about that. Now that you mention it, there might be something worthwhile in California. It's not Pennsylvania, but perhaps living there won't ruin my life entirely. There are so few interesting men here—it's a Herculean task to snag one. I mean, I nearly lost an eye at the last ball I attended—Evelyn Hall was determined to dance with Fred Haden, and no one was going to get in her way!" The two girls laughed.

"Yes, I bet you'll have to beat them back with a feather duster in California, you lucky thing." Candice sighed and leaned back in her chair, one hand resting across her forehead, no doubt picturing Christy surrounded by admiring cowboys.

Christy chuckled, "Perhaps you should move with me."

"I'd love to, only I'd never be allowed. I can't believe your parents gave you the choice. Mine never would."

"Well, I promise to write and tell you all about it. And if it is wonderful, maybe you'll find a way to join me."

"That sounds like a fine idea. Does your mother still insist on you becoming a teacher?"

"Yes." Christy's face turned gloomy. "She says I must make my own way in the world until I marry. I'm to study for my teaching certificate as soon as we get settled in San Francisco."

The next few weeks passed in a blur of activity. Christy and her parents packed their entire lives into boxes. Her beloved piano was sent to Hannigan's for sale at auction, along with the furnishings from the large old house on Maple Avenue where she'd spent her childhood years that weren't slated for use by prospective tenants. She shed tears over each piece as it was stacked into the back of a wagon before disappearing from view down the busy street.

She arranged her own clothing and other necessities in a small trunk, making sure to include her favorite old stuffed bear, given to her by her parents one Christmas years earlier. "Will we buy a new piano in San Francisco?" she asked as the wagon that held the rug-covered instrument rounded the bend and vanished.

"I'm sure we will," her mother replied. "I believe your father will be able to afford nice things in San Francisco, so don't fret over your old ones, my dear."

Christy folded her arms and walked back into the house. Their traveling trunks were piled in the foyer, almost blocking the front door, while the rooms were now practically bare. Her parents had decided to let the house, and the agent would be arriving later that afternoon to take down a description of the place. Two maids worked hard in the parlor, scrubbing and dusting, scouring and wiping—part of the extra help Mrs.

Hancock had hired for the last few days to help them pack and clean.

There was a knock at the door. Christy turned and opened it.

"Cab, Ma'am, for the train station." The driver of the cab they'd ordered stood on the stoop, hat in hand.

"Mam, the cab is here," called Christy.

"Oh, wonderful—the luggage is just over there, thank you." Mrs. Hancock indicated the trunks, and the driver hurried to carry them to his buggy. "Horace!" she yelled up the stairway.

"Yes, my dear, I'm here." He emerged from their bedroom, toting her hat box under one arm and an umbrella in the other.

"The cab is here, my dear."

"Good, he's right on time. Let's go then, shall we?"

The three of them took one last look around the hollow rooms of their home. Christy pinned her hat to her head as a piece of her heart tore away. She stepped outside and descended the stairs to the cab. As she climbed inside, she looked back out the window. They pulled away from the curb, and she watched the tall red brick building with the white trim fade into the distance. Her cheeks wet, she sank back onto the padded bench seat and drew a deep breath. She had a feeling that things would never be the same again.

Chapter Three

The steam train puffed loudly beside the platform. The sweeping dome of the Broad Street Station criss-crossed above the heads of Christy and her parents as they hurried toward the train. Porters led the way, expertly wheeling the Hancocks' luggage on wide trolleys, pitching it up into the carriage, and heaving it across their shoulders into the baggage car. The Hancocks followed close behind, climbing the stairs into a passenger car, where they located their assigned seats.

Christy sat by the window and stared out at the busy station. The engine let out another shrieking puff of steam. "Mam, did you remember to write to Aunt Penny in Ireland?"

"I did. I let her and Hank know we're moving, and that we'll inform them of our new address as soon as we get settled."

"I do wish we had some relatives nearer by. I would have loved to grow up with cousins, aunts and uncles around." Christy watched a family hurry down the platform together. They seemed to be searching for the correct train to board, each making sure the others were close by as they ran. The station housed more than a dozen tracks, all with trains huffing and rumbling to and from the platforms in a cacophony of clanking and hissing. Finally, the family located their carriage and leaped aboard just before the final whistle sounded.

"Yes, I know, my dear. I wish we could have given you siblings as well, but some things just aren't meant to be. Only the Good Lord knows why things happen the way they do. Perhaps you'll get to visit the family in Ireland someday."

"I would love to. I really don't remember anything about it, since I was only four when we left. I vaguely remember the journey to America on the ship, but I don't remember Ireland or the family at all."

Just then, their train blew a shrieking whistle. The noise echoed and bounced off the sloping walls of the station. A conductor on the platform, dressed in a smart black suit with silver buttons and a cap pulled low over his brow, cried, "All aboard, Topeka bound! All aboard!"

"I do believe we're off," said Mr. Hancock. He leaned forward to peer out the window.

The locomotive lurched, and after a few clanking heaves the pace smoothed out as the engine pulled the carriages from the station into the cold light of the gray winter's day.

As the train left Philadelphia, Christy looked at her family. Across from her, her mother was knitting, her brown hair swept up into a high bun. Daddy was settled next to Mam, his graying beard resting on the knot of the tie tucked into his buttoned vest. She thought back to the last time the family had taken a journey of the same magnitude together, when they'd emigrated from

Ireland fifteen years ago. That seems like an eternity ago, another lifetime.

The rail journey was a new experience for her, and for hours she relished watching the fields and woods flash by the window beside her as the train sped across the country. A green hollow filled with brilliantly-colored flowers filled her vision for a second, and she longed to be outside romping through it. She imagined their sweet scent filling her nostrils as the cool grass tickled her bare feet. At the very least, it would have been nice to stretch her legs after hours in her seat. A herd of lithe brown deer shied away from the noise of the train and bounded across the hollow, their soft wet noses raised high in the air.

There were large, still lakes covered with waterfowl, followed by deep dark woods holding unknown secrets and tall trees with trunks thicker than a dozen men standing together. She saw birds of every kind, white-tailed rabbits, and once a black bear foraging along the edge of the woods beside the tracks.

After a few days, though, the novelty of the journey wore off. She felt the lethargy that only utter boredom and the restrictions of a confined space for an extended amount of time could bring. Even the scenery had become tiresome, making her dizzy if she watched it for too long. She sighed and leaned back in her seat. "Mam, how long until we reach Topeka?" She knew how long, having already asked her mother half a dozen times. Topeka would be the next stop where they'd have a chance to get out of the train and take a decent walk.

"About four hours," answered her mother patiently. She'd taken a half-finished hat out of a bag at her feet and was carefully knitting a row of green pearl stitches across the top of it, her needles flying. "We should be in Missouri by now. Why don't you go to the dining car and grab some lunch? Your father and I will come with you if you like."

Christy's stomach growled, as if approving the suggestion. She rose to her feet and stretched her arms above her head with a great yawn.

Just then, the engine slowed, and she heard the screech of brakes as the locomotive pulled to a sudden stop. She grabbed the back of the seat to steady herself and looked up with joy. "Oh, are we stopping here?" She looked out the window at the dense woods beyond.

Her mother craned her neck, trying to see the front of the train. She looked stern. "Sit down, Christy," she whispered, her brow deeply furrowed. She placed her knitting carefully back into her bag and leaned over to whisper something to her husband.

Mr. Hancock nodded after a few seconds. "I'll go and check it out." He stood and straightened his suit vest, a frown forming above his bushy dark eyebrows. "You stay here, Christy, you hear me?"

Christy nodded. It was unlike her father to speak to her with such a firm manner. "What's happening, Mam?" she whispered. "Why have we pulled to a stop here in the middle of nowhere? I can't see a station platform anywhere. Is there something wrong?"

Christy's mother reached over and placed a hand on her arm. "I'm not sure. Just stay quiet."

After a few minutes had passed with no sign of Mr. Hancock's return, Mrs. Hancock had had enough of sitting still. "I'm going to see what's happened to your father. Promise me you won't move from this spot, my child."

Christy nodded again, her hands pressed together in her lap. While she waited patiently for her parents to return, she scanned up and down the side of the train. What is happening out there? The rest of the carriage was quiet. She sat as silent as everyone else, peering through the window, straining to discover anything about what was going on outside. But all she could see was a thicket of fir trees running parallel to the rails about twenty yards away. Beyond the tree line, there were only dark shadows. She stood for a moment to gaze out the windows on the opposite side of the train, but again all she saw were stout, unmoving fir trees lined up squarely one beside the other.

Suddenly gunshots rang out. They echoed back from the surrounding hills, filling the carriage with their sound. People spilled from their seats to duck under them.

Christy ran to the opposite window and peered out, craning her neck to see where the shots had come from. She gasped as she saw her parents being dragged from the train by dirty men in big hats, kerchiefs obscuring their faces. "Mam! Daddy!" she screamed against the glass.

The door of the carriage opened with a thud and one of the outlaws shoved his way in. He held a shotgun in his hands. "Listen up, everyone! I want yer valuables 'n yer cash. Hand it over. No one hasta get hurt. Just do as I'm askin' 'n ya'll all be on yer way shortly."

Christy couldn't move. She couldn't watch the man, her sights still fixed on her parents. They stood beside the train with one of the outlaws, his shotgun trained on them as he waited for his cronies.

The passengers scurried to comply, pulling money

from wallets and jewelry from luggage without leaving their hiding places. The man had taken off his hat and passed it around like a collection plate. He paused and stared at Christy above a greasy blue neckerchief. "Ya too, Miss."

She gaped at the window, unable to find her voice, unable to even turn her head.

He sneered at her, grunted in annoyance and strode from the carriage.

Soon the rest of the gang had finished scavenging the other carriages and jumped from the train. As the last one landed on the loam beside the tracks, the report of another weapon in the distance resounded throughout the valley. She heard a pack of horses galloping toward the train.

The outlaws ran to their own horses, shoving the loot into their saddlebags and pockets. They scrambled onto the beasts just as the local sheriff and his posse pulled into the clearing, firing haphazardly at the thieves. Returning their fire, the men tried to gallop away, but it was too late for some of them.

And then her father fell, red spreading across the pale skin of his forehead. Her mother collapsed a moment later.

Christy stopped praying—she hadn't even known she was—and began screaming. She dropped to her knees, unable to do otherwise, unable to stop her voice, unable to stop the horror of her parents' deaths in the crossfire from playing across her eyes—

—SLAP! She blinked, and found herself standing, the conductor gripping her arm with one hand, the other raised in case she still needed more rousing. "Are you all right, young lady?" he bellowed.

She was only able to manage a shake of her head. No, she was most certainly not all right.

"Do you know those folks?" He pointed out the window.

"My parents," she squeaked.

His eyes widened and he let his free hand drop. "Come with me." He led her out of the carriage and down the stairs to where her parents lay. Three outlaws also lay dead on the ground; the rest, along with the posse, were long gone.

She walked, then crawled on hands and knees to her parents. She pressed one hand onto each of them and hung her head, letting the tears drip from her cheeks to the earth below. She smoothed her mother's hair and patted her father's chest as a sob escaped her and her entire body shook. "Noooo," she wailed. Laying her head on the ground, she sobbed into the dirt.

"I'm so sorry," the conductor mumbled behind her.

Chapter Four

That night, Christy stared out the window, her face a blank. She leaned her head against the glass, and it bumped with every clack of the train on the tracks. Her eyes were red-rimmed and watery, her throat burned.

She still hadn't been able to process everything that had happened. She couldn't believe that Mam and Daddy were gone, their bodies left behind in some town in Missouri. She was all alone in the world, trundling through wild, untamed country.

They passed through never-ending prairies, tall grasses swaying beside the tracks and the furry brown backs of buffalo peppering the undulating plains in patches. Apart from the buffalo, there was nothing to see but long open stretches of gray-green grass and the occasional bird hovering on an updraft.

Overcome with grief and exhaustion, her eyes shuttered closed.

The slam of the compartment door woke Christy. She stirred, pushed her loosened hair from her face and jolted upright in her seat. What had roused her?

She stood, opened the door and saw the back of a boy disappear down the aisle of the train and out the carriage door.

Instinctively, she pulled her mother's bag to her chest and opened it to look inside. Mrs. Hancock's pocketbook was gone, along with her jewelry box. Her mother had stashed them in a small box in her handbag to keep them safe. And now they were gone. She dropped it and reached for her father's briefcase, now open with the latch flapping loosely. Opening it, she gasped. Her father's wallet was gone, along with a few paper bonds.

She dropped the briefcase on the seat beside her and covered her face with her hands. Anything of value her parents had left behind had been taken. She had nothing.

Just then, she heard the conductor walk past. She opened the door again and waved him over. "Excuse me, sir."

He halted. "Yes, miss, how can I help you?"

"A boy ran through the carriage just now and out that door. Did you see him?"

"No, I don't believe I did."

"He stole my…my money and jewelry. He took everything I have left. You have to find him, please."

The conductor's face blanched. "Oh dear, I am sorry. Are you sure?"

"Yes, very sure." Christy rubbed her face and sighed deeply. "Please, can you help me?"

The conductor nodded his head quickly, "I certainly will, Miss. After what you've been through, I owe you that." He spun on his heel and trotted down the aisle and out the door the boy had disappeared through only moments earlier.

Christy watched him go, then gathered all the hand luggage to herself and looped her arms and legs through the straps, keeping it as close as she could. She would be careful to guard it more closely now—though it was already too late.

Meredith hurried down the Topeka train platform, calling for the train to stop as it hopped forward. She pulled her hat from her head and waved it frantically at the brakeman, hoping to catch his attention, but the locomotive wouldn't stop. The engine edged forward, chugging and chuffing loudly, and was soon on its way.

She stumbled to a halt. "Darn it!" she exclaimed as she realized she'd missed the train and would need to wait until the following day to visit her sister in Kansas City. In her late forties, she wasn't used to exerting herself in such a way. It took her a few minutes to get her breath back.

She fanned her reddened face with a handheld fan as she gazed around the platform. "Well, I suppose I just wasn't meant to get on that train today," she said to herself. "At least Morty will be pleased to see me home again, knowing I can make him a hot dinner rather than the cold cuts and bread I left out for him."

She was about to trot down the steps at the end of the platform and head back into town when she heard a wailing noise behind her. Who could that be, making such a wretched sound? She turned to see a young woman with a head of glossy red curls doubled over on a bench on the platform, weeping as though she'd just lost everything in the world. She hurried over to the girl. "Whatever's happened, my dear?"

The poor dear was barely able to stand up straight,

even with Meredith's arm to help her. With her entire body shaking, Christy Hancock, recently of Philadelphia, recounted her whole sorry story.

Meredith listened with growing alarm. "And what are you doing in Topeka?" she finally asked. "Do you know anyone here?"

Christy burst into tears again, and Meredith handed her a handkerchief to dry her eyes. "No. I don't know anyone, anywhere except Philadelphia! My living relatives are all in Ireland. Only Mam, Daddy and I came across to start a new life here!" She let out another wail before blowing her nose. "All I have left of them now is some of their luggage and a letter my Mam sent me months ago when I was staying with a friend. It was stashed in my trunk. I've tucked it into my sleeve so I can read it when I miss them. I figured Topeka was as good a place as any for me to be. That miserable train… I couldn't stay on board for one moment longer!"

"Of course," Meredith said, wrapping her arm around the girl. "So you have nowhere to go, no warm bed to spend the night in?"

Christy shook her head. "I've got no one and nothing. I've barely anything in the world to call my own, just my luggage and Mam and Daddy's. A thief stole their pocketbooks and valuables. We left our home in Pennsylvania to move to California…and now I've nowhere to go-o-o-o!"

"Well, my dear, you must come home with me."

Christy looked up, still sniffling. "Oh, do you really mean that? That's awfully kind of you, but I don't want to be a burden to you…"

"Nonsense. The only burden would be my worrying about you sleeping out in the street! Come now and I'll show you my home and settle you in. My name's Meredith Poke. And my husband, Morty, will be pleased to have you as well!"

Dearest Candy:

I know that I've been remiss in my correspondence. I promised to write you as soon as we got to California, so I know you will be worried about me. I'm writing now to let you know that I'm in Topeka, Kansas. We never made it to California as planned.

I find that I can't hold back the tears as I write this, so please forgive the smudges. Mam and Daddy are dead. They were killed by outlaws who held up and robbed our train. I disembarked alone in Topeka, and kindly strangers, Meredith Poke and her husband Morton, have taken me in and given me a place to stay.

I'm sure you're shocked at the news. I must admit that I'm finding it very hard to write down. We haven't been able to hold a real funeral, since their bodies are being held by the Missouri State Police as part of their investigation into the incident. As it stands, I don't know anyone in Topeka who would come to their funeral anyway. I couldn't even make my way back to Philadelphia to put together a funeral—a thief stole their valuables and I have no money for a ticket. All I have to my name are my trunk of clothes, some of their mementos and my silly old stuffed bear.

I'm sorry to lay all this at your feet, but I don't have anyone else to talk to about it. Oh, how I wish you were here with me. I miss you so.

The Pokes' home is a cozy cottage in a growing part of town. The house, they tell me, is built from a pre-fabricated frame, as are so many of the homes in this area. They have given me their guest room. I have been here for three days now and feel most welcome. I don't know how long I can stay, but I hope they will let me remain until I can sort out a way to access Mam and Daddy's bank account so that I can get together the money to return home.

After that, I have no idea what I will do. Perhaps I will teach after all. I'm sure I won't be able to afford to move back into the house—it has likely been rented by a family by now. But I should be able to find some lodgings on a teacher's wage, don't you think?

I feel completely alone in the world, as though the ground has been pulled out from beneath my feet and I am falling, falling… I'm so grateful that at least I can write to you about it. I know you will understand what I am feeling.

Please, please, please write to me at the enclosed address. If I am not here, hopefully Meredith will forward your letters to me wherever I end up.

Kindest regards,
Christy

Christy lay the quill down on the table blotter, sighed and wiped the moisture from her cheeks with a bunched-up white handkerchief. With a sniffle, she stood to her feet and folded the paper into an envelope. "Meredith?" she called.

Meredith peeked around the kitchen door. Her apron was dusted with flour and she held a mixing bowl in her hands with the long handle of a wooden spoon jutting from it. "Yes, dear?"

Christy reached for her coat and buttoned it over her green calico dress. She smoothed her hair and pinned on a hat. "I'm going to the post office. I have to stop by the bank as well, so I might be a while."

"All right, dear. Will you be home in time for supper?"

"Yes, thank you. I'm sorry I won't be here to help you prepare it, but I promise to clean up afterward."

"That's fine, dear. I'll see you then."

Christy hurried out, the letter in her coat pocket. Her boots slapped loudly against the hard earth, and the hem of her gown dusted the ground as she walked. Topeka was a bustling city, and she watched with interest as cowboys rode by on the backs of sturdy broncos and housewives bustled down sidewalks dragging unruly children in their wake. A covered wagon trundled by, kicking up dust with its spoked wheels and pulling a trotting mule along behind it.

She mailed her letter at the main post office, then made her way to Topeka National Bank down the street. As she stepped from the boardwalk onto the road at a corner, her left foot landed in a muddy puddle. Water seeped through the laces of her boots, wetting her stockinged foot in an instant. She grimaced, leaped from the puddle and shook her foot, but the damage was done. She groaned and hurried into the bank.

"Can I help you, ma'am?" An obliging teller leaned

forward and peered down at Christy over round spectacles. He smiled at her, taking in her curvaceous figure and fine features in a single glance.

"Yes, thank you. I'd like to make a withdrawal, but the account I need to access is in Philadelphia. So I guess I may need to do a wire transfer first. I'm not really sure how all of this works."

"Of course, I can set that up for you. Do you have your account details?"

"Yes, I do." Christy pulled the paperwork she'd found in her father's luggage from her coat pocket and handed it over.

The teller quickly scribbled some notes, then handed the papers back. "Thank you, ma'am. This could take a few days, so how about you come back in then?"

"All right, I'll be by again in a few days." Christy smiled at the teller, then headed back to the Pokes' house.

When she arrived, Meredith hurried to meet her at the door. "Oh Christy dear, I'm glad you're home. A telegram came for you from Philadelphia while you were gone. I think it's from that lawyer you were trying to reach."

Christy removed her coat and hat and took the paper Meredith held out for her. She read it quickly, sighed in relief and pressed the paper to her chest with a smile. "Thank you, Meredith. Yes, it is from Mr. Smythe. He says they have read Daddy's will and he left everything to me. He's going to coordinate with Daddy's bank in Philadelphia to wire me some money via the bank here. Oh, this is good news. I knew it would happen, but to see it in writing is a relief."

Meredith beamed. "I'm so glad for you, my dear. I

know it doesn't help your grief, but at least you won't be destitute."

"Well, I should have enough money to support myself for a little while. I'll have to find work eventually, since Daddy's money won't last forever. Perhaps I should continue on to California like we'd planned—I know there are a lot of job opportunities out there. Or, maybe I should go back to Philly. I think that's what I'd rather do—after all, my friends are there, even if I don't have family there any longer."

"Well, let's have a nice slice of chocolate cake tonight for dessert to celebrate small mercies." Meredith patted Christy's hand and walked back to the kitchen where she'd been mixing cake batter in a large wooden bowl.

Christy followed her, drawing a deep breath through her nose. "Mmmm, that smells divine. What's for dinner?"

"Bacon, greens and cornbread."

Christy's stomach growled loudly and she laughed. "Well, I guess I'm hungry. I'll set the table."

Chapter Five

"I do hope my aunt and uncle in Ireland write back soon," Christy remarked as she and Meredith strolled down the street to the bank.

"I'm sure they were saddened to hear your news, my dear."

"I know Mam was close to Aunt Penny when they were younger, but we haven't seen them in so many years. It's been weeks since I wrote—surely there will be a letter today."

"Well, by the time we get home, no doubt the mail will have arrived at the house. We will see then."

The two women stepped into the bank through the arched stone doorway and walked across the cold floor and to where the teller was counting coins into a bag. He peered at them over his spectacles with a grin. "So I see that you've returned, Miss Hancock."

"Yes, sir. Have you received the wire transfer from the bank in Philadelphia? You said it would only take a few days and it's been weeks…"

"Well, there is unfortunately something of an issue there." He stopped counting and pushed the bag to one side, giving them his full attention. "It seems there is another claim on your late father's estate."

"What? What does that mean?" Christy's eyes widened and she tilted her head to the side, her red curls drooping across her shoulder.

"It means that I can't give you any money today. I'm sorry, Miss Hancock. I don't know the particulars of the case, only that the bank in Philadelphia won't release the funds because they're disputed. You'll have to contact your attorney to find out more, I'm afraid."

Christy faced Meredith, her face pale. "Oh dear. I wonder who it could be."

"Well, I suppose we'll find out soon enough. There's nothing more we can do here—let's go home and see if your lawyer has written. If not, you can always send him a wire." Meredith looped her arm through Christy's and led her from the building.

Christy stared at the ground as they walked, her heart racing. What did it all mean? Was she destined to be left completely alone without a cent to her name? What would she do?

Her mind numb, she stared at a passing stagecoach, watching it to the end of the street. There was a shiny new steam locomotive sitting dormant at the station, a cloud of mist billowing from its stack. It wasn't long ago she had boarded a train just like that and her life had changed forever. The memory of it overwhelmed her, and she choked back the tears.

Meredith looked at her with concern, squeezing her hand. "There, there, my dear. I'm sure it's just a misunderstanding of some kind. After all, your parents had no other heirs, did they?"

"None. I don't know who could be claiming otherwise. It's just that… I feel as though I've been forsaken—by my parents, my friends, perhaps even God. Everything is such a mess."

Meredith sighed and pulled Christy to her in an embrace. "God has not forsaken you, and your parents didn't either. Have you tried praying about it?"

Christy shook her head against Meredith's shoulder and sniffled.

"Well, maybe you should. This is all part of growing up, my dear. Sometimes we have to face hard things, and it might seem as though nothing is going our way. But these are the moments in life that shape us. How we react to trials and hardships tell us what we're truly made of."

Christy lifted her head and nodded. Meredith handed her a clean handkerchief from a dress pocket, and Christy blew her nose into it, then offered it back.

"No, thank you, dear—you can keep it."

"Thank you." Christy tucked it into her sleeve and they continued down the street, arm in arm.

When they reached the house, Christy ran to check the mailbox. She pulled several letters from it and flicked through them. One was addressed to her, and she held it up for Meredith to see. "From my lawyer!"

"See, what did I tell you? Let's find out what this kerfuffle is all about."

They bustled inside and Meredith began boiling water in the kettle for coffee. Christy sat at the dining table and placed the letter in front of her, staring at it until Meredith placed a steaming cup of coffee beside it. Christy reached for the cup, took a sip, and only then opened the letter:

Sterling, Brite and Smythe, Attorneys at Law
Suite 12, 102 Evans Road
Philadelphia, PA

Dear Miss Hancock,

We are writing to inform you that there has been a claim made against the estate of your late father, Mr. Horace Hancock.

When we telegrammed Mr. Hank and Mrs. Penelope Jones of Bangor, Ireland to let them know of your parents' demise (at your father's request), they responded immediately to claim that Mrs. Jones, as the sister and sister-in-law to the deceased, is the rightful heir to the estate. She claims also to be your guardian and insists that you return to Ireland to live with her and her husband.

At this stage, the court has ordered the assets of the estate frozen until such time as said claim can be investigated. This means that you will not be able to access the funds or assets of the estate until the court has determined that they are rightfully yours.

It is our belief, as your counsel, that the claim made is without merit. However, if the claimants decide to pursue the matter further, it may be some months before a decision is made.

We will contact you as soon as we know more.

Best regards,
Harris Sterling and William Smythe

Christy folded the letter and pushed it back into the

envelope, her lips quivering. "Some months? How can I wait that long? I can't… I haven't got enough money for train fare home. And even if I did, where would I stay? Oh dear, what can I do?"

Meredith patted Christy's back, her lips tight. "I must say, it's frightful that your own family would do this to you—leaving you out here all alone without a penny. And really, what makes them think they stand to inherit anything from your parents? It's an affront, is what it is."

Christy had never heard Meredith get angry before, and she half-grinned through her tears. "Meredith… you've been so kind to me. And now I can't repay you. I was hoping I'd be able to stay a little longer and pay board. But now I don't know what to do."

"Well, never you mind about board. You can stay here until you get yourself sorted out, my dear. Morty and I consider the help you give me around the house more than enough to compensate."

Christy embraced Meredith, her mind racing. She would have to stay with the Pokes a while longer, but she knew she couldn't intrude on them forever. And the teacher's exam cost more than she could afford, so that would have to wait too. It was time to form a new plan and fast.

Chapter Six

June 1889

The problem with being part of the Indian Territory land rush, Brent Taylor mused, was the timing. Couldn't do spring planting when you didn't get your acreage until the end of April.

But then, he'd only ever planted a kitchen garden before, having been raised on a Kentucky horse ranch where breeding and selling steeds provided the family's livelihood. It had cost him a lot of money to relocate and set up outside the new town of Newton in the Indian Territory, which meant it would take more time—and money—to establish his own breeding program here.

So he'd decided to try farming first. This year he was going to plant crops—several acres of short-season corn now, along with some cabbage, salad greens and chicory, and winter wheat and oats come autumn. He'd also invested in a dozen hens, so he'd have eggs for the time being. If all worked out, he could afford a small herd of beef cattle next year or the year after, and have fodder for them besides. Down the road, he could get back to raising horses.

One advantage to the Oklahoma land rush, though, was that everyone was in the same pickle calendar-wise, so they all helped each other out. Two days ago, he'd been part of a barn-raising for his neighbor, Clive Harris. Now Clive was driving a pair of Clydesdales across his front meadow, plowing up the land for corn.

Brent sprang down the steps of his new one-story ranch house and waved to Clive, then noticed the rest of the Harrises following behind him in an open wagon—including Kip, Clive's teenage son, whom Brent often hired to help out around the ranch. Then another wagon filled with folks came into view and turned in at his gate, towing a second plow. What was going on?

He lifted a hand to shield his eyes from the rising morning sun and peered down the driveway. It was the Connellys, from the property directly west of his, and the Hattons from the south, closer to town. The three families waved, and he could hear a soft melody floating across the fields, as they sang their way up the winding drive. "Well, I'll be darned." He slapped his thighs as the wagons reached the house. "What in blazes is going on here?" he asked with a grin.

"We heard some greenhorn was fixin' to grow his first crop and we thought we'd better mosey on down and offer a hand." Ed Connelly chewed a long piece of grass and squinted at Brent through small brown eyes. "Can't have you killin' yourself or your first crop, now can we?"

"I sure do appreciate it." Brent's heart swelled as Mr. Hatton vaulted from his wagon and the men helped the women and children from their wagon beds. "I'm awful sorry, but I wasn't expecting so many of you. I haven't a mite of food in the house." He took his hat from his head and twisted it in his hands.

"Never mind about that," said Mary Connelly, smiling genially at him. "We've brought everything we need." She lifted two large picnic baskets from the back of the wagon and handed them to her children to carry inside, then hauled out loaves of freshly baked bread wrapped in linens, jars of preserves and pickles and an assortment of other covered dishes.

"Wow, that looks amazing. You folks are too kind." Brent watched them all traipse into his house with full arms.

"Leave the womenfolk to their business, Brent—let's get you to plowin'." Clive grinned and stepped back behind the plow handles.

Brent nodded and mounted Patty to hurry ahead of the teams and show them where to go. He'd already plowed the fields once, and dark earth showed up through wisps of upturned grassroots. Birds dove and pecked at the grubs and worms making their way to the surface. The men quickly got to work, tilling the field in long straight lines, turning it over a second time to find the moist soil beneath. Kip and some of the older boys walked behind them, carrying the seed on their backs in large hessian shoulder bags. They tossed it into the furrows and kicked dirt over it.

The warming sun kissed their limbs and they sang as they worked. Brent remembered what it felt like to be part of a family, and he missed his parents and Annabelle more than ever. He'd become accustomed to the ache of loneliness. But now, with happy chatter and warm smiles all around him, he felt for a moment as though he weren't alone in the world, and he liked the sensation.

When the day's work was done, Brent and the other men went inside to wash up for supper. They'd all picnicked outside for lunch, eating thick slices of cold beef and bread and drinking cool water drawn from the nearby creek. Brent was looking forward to the last meal of the day, since he'd been smelling it all afternoon—the scent of good food had wafted out to the fields where they worked.

He strode into the dining room, looking around the crowded kitchen with pleasure. He hadn't had much chance to keep the new place clean, and was glad the visitors had straightened up, making the room glow with warmth and homeliness.

The table was set with a glazed ham, green beans, creamed potatoes, moist cornbread alongside a golden cake of butter, black-eyed peas, carrots and plenty of greens. Brent's mouth watered at the sight of it. He hadn't seen that much food in one place since the last family Christmas at his parents' ranch in 1887—before his father and mother died, before the heartbreak of staying had gotten too much and he'd sold it all to start over elsewhere…

He shook himself, smacked his lips and sat with the rest of the group. The children sat wherever they could find a place in the living room, on kitchen stools and on the floor.

"Would you say the blessing please, Brent?" asked Mary.

"Of course." Everyone bowed their heads. "Heavenly Father, thank You for this food and the hands that prepared it. Thank You for kindly neighbors and rich farmland…and new beginnings. Bless all we eat to our bodies. Amen."

"Amen," the chorus resounded, and Brent beamed at the sound of it. He liked having a house with noise in it again. He'd had too much quiet of late, and was worried he'd almost forgotten how to socialize.

Those around the table quietly passed the dishes, sharing with those around them. The women bustled between the rooms, serving steaming spoonfuls of the delicious food onto the plates of hungry children and making sure everyone's cups were full to the brim with strong coffee, cool spring water or—for a few of the men—Kentucky sipping whiskey.

Brent took an enormous bite of warm cornbread dripping in butter and smiled. Thank you, God, for good friends.

Chapter Seven

"Oh God, I don't truly believe that You've abandoned me, honestly I don't. I don't know why I said that and I'm sorry I did. It just seems as though nothing will go right for me, like I've lost everything in this world that there is to lose. I could really use Your help. Please, would You show me a way forward? I just don't know what to do." Christy unfolded her hands, opened her eyes and stood to her feet beside her neatly made bed.

Summer was well underway and she was no closer to finding a solution to her problems. Her father's will was still being contested, she still had no job or money to speak of, and even the letters from Candice, brimming with tearful encouragement, were no longer able to buoy her flagging spirits.

She regarded her reflection in the looking glass, smoothed her hair and pinched her pale cheeks. Then she trudged down the stairs to breakfast.

Meredith and Morty greeted her warmly as she sat at the dining table in their small kitchen. Though the food smelled delicious, she had no appetite. Morty smiled at her, his well-waxed handlebar moustache framing his wide mouth. His thinning hair was combed evenly across his scalp and his gray eyes twinkled happily. "Come now, my dear, you'll fade away," he said, handing her some toasted bread.

"I just can't seem to eat much." She did nibble slowly on the bread.

Meredith and Morty looked at each other. Meredith's hair was curled into a tight bun at the back of her head and she wore a plain brown dress and white pinafore with small red rosebuds splashed across it. "Christy dear, we have to talk to you about your future," she began. "We'd like you to stay here with us. As you know, our children are grown with families of their own, and our house has been awfully quiet ever since they left."

Christy stopped eating. "I would love to stay here. Your house is very warm and welcoming." She smiled at the couple.

The pair looked at each other again before Meredith continued speaking. "But you're a young woman, and like our own children you should be out in the world, starting a family of your own. You just don't seem… happy. We worry about you."

Christy looked at her plate. Now her appetite had left entirely. "Oh," she said.

"Dear, we don't mean to upset you," Meredith said quickly, reaching over to pat Christy's arm. "Of course you can stay here as long as you need. We just don't want you to be stuck here all on your lonesome. I'll tell you what—why don't I help you write letters to your friends back home? You can reach out to them and see who might offer you money or lodging. Maybe something will come up—you never know until you ask."

Christy nodded. "That sounds like a good idea."

"We're happy to help you in whatever way we can, you know that," said Morty. "We just don't want you to lose hope."

"Thank you," Christy whispered, a wave of grief and loneliness filling her heart. She stared out the window at the brilliant flowers in the front garden as they waved in the summer breeze. It seemed to her that hope had been lost a long time ago.

The weeks passed quickly, and Christy's heart began healing. She enjoyed her time with Meredith and Morty and had slipped seamlessly into sharing their comfortable life with them. But she hadn't heard anything hopeful from her friends back in Philadelphia concerning a possible job or place to stay. "I'm beginning to think no one cares at all!" she said one morning to Meredith while they made her bed together. "Another day without a single letter!"

"Give it some more time, my dear," Meredith said. "It can take a while for people to sort things out."

Christy shoved the corner of the sheet beneath her mattress and straightened it despondently. "It's as though no one's concerned that I've been left all alone. They don't even write to express their sorrow at Mam and Daddy's passing. Candy is the only one who's written back, and she can't convince her parents to let me stay with them." She thought she might cry just thinking about it. She straightened her back and smoothed her dress.

"Just wait a little longer," Meredith said gently. "It hasn't been so very long." But she knew that if help was likely to come from Philadelphia, it would've arrived already. She just didn't want to say so to Christy. The poor girl would need to make other plans for her life. "Why don't you come to the mercantile with me? You can help me pick out the ingredients for dessert tonight?"

Christy brightened a little. Nodding, she said, "That would be wonderful. I need something to take my mind off my troubles and you know how I love to bake."

The Fair Deal General Store was a bright, cheerful place, its shelves lined with groceries, linens, fabrics, shoes and farming supplies. A person could find whatever he or she might need and even a few things they never knew they wanted within its hewn-timber walls—and what they couldn't, they could order specially. It was Christy's favorite place in Topeka outside of the Pokes' home, reminding her of Wanamaker's huge store back in Philadelphia where she and her mother used to shop, only smaller.

At the entrance to the store was a notice board holding flyers about various happenings around town, or missing and lost items. One particular stack of cream-colored flyers with thick black lettering caught Meredith's eye. "Christy, dear," she said, turning the young woman around so that she didn't see the board. "My back is aching a little—could you go fetch the rest of the ingredients while I speak with the clerk for a moment?"

"Of course, Meredith," Christy beamed. "I'll take care of everything."

Meredith watched Christy leave, then turned back to face the notice board. Yes, she had seen right—there in big, bold letters were the words:

Mail-Order Brides Wanted!

Meredith inched closer so she could read the small

print beneath the heading. She'd forgotten her spectacles, and it was becoming so bad that she couldn't read a line without squinting these days. The flyer was for an information night to be held the following Tuesday, and encouraged local young women to come and learn more about becoming a mail-order bride.

It seemed that Destiny had placed the notice there for her to see. Why, this could be just the thing to get Christy out of danger! Her eyes widened as she read the rest of the note. There were men out West who wanted brides right away. Christy could be one of them. She's pretty enough to make any man happy!

Meredith glanced over her shoulder to make sure Christy was still busy elsewhere, then took a flyer and stuffed it in her pocket. I'll wait for the right moment, then tell her about it. But I think our prayers may have been answered!

That afternoon, as Christy helped Meredith bake a yellow cake with chocolate frosting for dessert, Meredith asked, as casually as she could manage, "Christy, my dear, have you thought about what you might do if your friends don't reply to your correspondence?"

Christy sifted flour into the bowl. "Mam wanted me to sit the teaching examination, but now I can't afford to. Why?"

"Christy, you're a woman full grown—old enough to make decisions for yourself. What is it you want to do?"

"I don't know. I'm nineteen years old, but I don't feel grown. I don't want to be on my own, but I'm really too old for anyone to take me in and care for me. And yet I feel as though I'm too young to support myself." She sighed. "I really don't know what I want—only that I feel lonely and lost."

"You're old enough to marry, my dear."

Christy's eyes stretched wide. "Marry? Meredith, who would I marry? I don't know any unmarried men out here. I mean, I see men around town and I say 'good day' to them, but I don't really know any well enough to marry." She looked at the floor, her cheeks flushed red.

Meredith straightened her back and dusted the flour from her hands. "You only need to know one, Christy. And you just haven't met the right one yet, is all."

"Do you think I will find someone someday, Meredith?"

"Of course you will, my dear—as sweet and pretty as you are." She reached into her pocket, took out the flyer and handed it to Christy. "And there are men out there looking."

Christy's eyebrows arched as she read the sheet. "Why… I could never do such a thing! Marry a man I've never met?"

Meredith's face turned serious. "You don't have to if you don't want to, my dear. But this might be your best option. I'm afraid none of your friends are going to help you, and you can't count on your family in Ireland. The men in this program are supposed to be good men—it says here that they've all been interviewed and vetted. At least go to the meeting and ask them about it. They might help put your mind to ease."

Christy nodded. "Okay. I will go to the meeting. But I can't imagine tying myself to a man I've never met."

"Perhaps a family is what you're really searching for. You feel lonely, afraid, uncertain of what to do. A husband could be the answer to your prayers."

Christy pondered Meredith's words. It was true—she missed having a family. She didn't want to live on her own, and she didn't know how to make her own way in the world without a penny to fall back on. Yes, she would go to the meeting and see what they had to say. There wasn't any harm in finding out more.

Chapter Eight

Bonnie McCloud was a pretty middle-aged woman with blonde hair, brown eyes and as thick an Irish accent as Christy's mother. In fact, from outside the church meeting hall, the woman's voice sounded so much like Mrs. Hancock that Christy froze in the darkness. She was already nervous enough about the meeting, and needed a few moments to regain her composure. She sat down on a stone wall beside the church gate to think.

Maybe she should turn around and head back to Meredith and Morty's place—this whole idea was ridiculous. Who marries someone they've never even seen before? But if she didn't do this, what was she to do? She had no one to turn to, nowhere to go. She couldn't continue the journey to California or become a teacher—she didn't have the money—and even if she could, she'd still be alone in the world. However, she could put her fate in God's hands and pray that she'd be matched with a good man who could give her a warm and loving home.

Christy stood to her feet, dusted off the back of her skirt and walked into the church hall. Mrs. McCloud was already telling the young women sitting on folding chairs about the mail-order bride program, so she hurried over to an empty chair and sat, smoothing the front of her dress and folding her hands in her lap.

"... The men we match you with are all checked carefully by one of our offices. They're each interviewed and have to provide character references from people who know them. I can assure you, they are hard-working and can provide for a family. And they'll pay for you to travel out to meet them. These men want to get married, but there aren't a lot of women out West. Many towns have no women of marrying age at all.

"Of course, you're free to return to Topeka if you don't wish to go ahead with it once you arrive, but I would encourage you all to give it a try. We have placed hundreds of girls like you throughout the West, and most are happily married, raising beautiful families in their new homes. They write to tell us how much their new situations suit them, and they are usually well pleased with their husbands."

Christy listened with interest. Maybe this would be a good option for her after all—a home with a loving husband and a family of her own. Hearing about it stirred a longing deep in her heart that had been buried when her parents died months ago. She wiped stray tears from beneath her eyes.

At the end, she stood with the others to pack the folding chairs away, then joined the line of girls in front of Bonnie who wanted to sign up. When it was her turn, she gave Mrs. McCloud her name and details. But after everyone else was done, she asked to speak to her in private, and confessed her misgivings about the scheme.

"The men in the program are thoroughly checked, Miss Hancock—the agency makes sure they all have enough income to support a family, no criminal history, no dissipating habits. They're good men."

What about love? Christy thought. The agency can do nothing to ensure I'll actually love the man they match me with, or he me. What does money mean if we have no feelings, no attraction, to each other? But she was too embarrassed to talk about such a thing as love with the older woman. Mrs. McCloud would probably think her immature to even consider such things. After all, the way she'd spoken of it, marrying was about finding a home and security, not romance. That's what her mother had always told her as well.

She dare not ask for anything more than that. Perhaps she wasn't even supposed to. Mam had often told her to get her head out of the clouds, that marriage wasn't a fairy tale and that she would do well to settle for a good man who could provide for her. So that's what Christy had prayed for over the years.

But the things she asked for, even prayed for, were quite different from what she truly wanted. It felt like a lifetime since the incidents on the train. She had done a lot of growing in the meantime, but inside she was still that girl who watched the fields of flowers passing by the train window, daydreaming about the things she'd left behind and what was to come.

Mam's voice rang loudly in her memories: "Christy, if you can find a man who's honorable, a good provider and will take care of you, you can't ask for better than that. Love is a luxury most women can ill afford. Daydreams will leave you cold and lonely, my girl."

So the following morning when Christy awoke, she dressed quickly and looked at herself solemnly in the mirror. She took a deep breath, ran down the stairs and said to Meredith, "I'm ready. I'm getting married."

Within three days, everything was organized. Christy had been matched with one Brent Taylor, a farmer in the Indian Territory. Not that far west of Topeka after all—more south than west, really. Compared to going to California, it would be a short trip.

Mrs. McCloud gave her a letter that Mr. Taylor had written to greet his future bride. In it, he said that he'd been lonely ever since his fiancée had died three years earlier in a riding accident. More recently, his parents had passed on, leaving him completely alone on the extensive property in Kentucky he'd inherited from them. He'd decided to sell it and start a new life in the West, recently claiming forty acres in the Unassigned Lands of the Indian Territory near a town called Newton.

So he's an orphan too, Christy thought. *At least he'll know some of my pain. We'll have that in common.*

She picked up her quill, dipped it in the inkwell and held it poised above the blank sheet of paper on the table in front of her. What should she write to a man she'd never met, but whom she would soon be married to?

Dear Mr. Taylor,

I was so very pleased to hear from you. Thank you for sharing with me about your family. I too have lost my parents and understand what it is like to be alone in the world.

From your description, your new ranch sounds lovely. I don't have much experience with country life, having spent most of my childhood in Philadelphia. We did have a chicken coop in our backyard, but otherwise I don't know much about caring for animals.

You asked me what I like to do. I love to play piano, garden, bake and read.

Mrs. McCloud is arranging for me to travel to you next week, so you will no doubt receive this letter shortly before I arrive. I look forward to meeting you at the train station. I have bright red hair—that may help you recognize me.

Kind regards,
Christy Hancock

Mr. Taylor's letter had stated that he would meet Christy at the station with a bunch of daisies on the day arranged for her to arrive. She shut her eyes as she folded it and placed it in her luggage, next to the letter from her mother. She took her own letter to Brent and placed it in an envelope, ready to mail.

She hadn't been certain about going through with the marriage at first, but the more she thought about it, the more she knew it was her best option. She had no money and no way to get her hands on any for several months. The Pokes had been kind to put her up for so long, but she couldn't impose on their hospitality any longer. It was time for her to move on, and marrying Mr. Taylor seemed the only viable option.

The following week, Christy was in her room packing her bags. She held her cherished stuffed bear to her cheek a moment, then shoved it into the trunk. It was time to leave for Newton and she was nervous, tapping her foot while she packed.

Meredith walked in and greeted her with a smile, carrying a pile of clothing. She laid it down on the bed beside Christy. “Here you go, my dear. I know they’re not much, but these ought to get you by for a little while in your new place.”

Christy still had the luggage she had brought with her from Philadelphia, but it was mostly gowns and fancier items. These work clothes would give her enough to last a good while in her new home. “Thank you, Meredith.” Her throat tightened with emotion as she considered all the kindly woman had done for her.

“Don’t mention it, my dear. They belonged to my daughters, and now they’ll find a good second home with you. I know you’ll look after them. Now let’s get you down to the station.”

Morty came in and helped carry Christy’s luggage out to the waiting wagon, where they loaded everything and climbed up onto the bench seat. The drive to the station was quiet as each of them contemplated what lay ahead. Christy felt the tension travel from the pit of her stomach up her back, causing her neck to stiffen.

“I do hope we won’t be late,” said Meredith, holding tightly to the rattling wagon seat.

They made it in time, but the loud whistle of the train gave Christy a jolt. Meredith uttered a prayer of thanks. They hurried to get Christy’s luggage to the brakeman, who loaded it on board. Then she turned to face the couple. “Thank you for everything,” she said, grasping the older woman’s hands in hers. “I shall never forget the kindness you showed me at the worst moment of my life.”

Meredith wiped away the tears spilling down her face as Morty waved goodbye.

Christy stepped onto the train and took a deep breath to steel herself for the journey ahead. It was her first time on a train since the robbery. She sat in the first compartment she found as her legs were threatening to give way beneath her. On the platform, she saw Meredith and Morty and waved again, her heart heavy with the sorrow of bidding goodbye to the couple she'd grown so fond of. She prayed she could reward their faith in her and do them proud in such a tough world.

Chapter Nine

Most days, Brent would have been tending to the daily business of running his farm. But the 29th of July was different—it was for quiet solitude. On that day every year, Brent took a break from the work that would normally consume his waking hours and spent time alone, remembering the past and thinking about what might have been.

He led his horse to the empty field behind the ranch house and tied it to a fence post, then took off his broad-brimmed black riding hat and placed it against his chest. A moment's silence to remember Annabelle. In previous years, he would have done this in the place where she'd died, his gaze sweeping across the pasture where the thunderstorm hit, the rocks where she fell to her death.

Now he was in a new place, a new field, but the dull thud of her head hitting the ground still resounded in his ears. He closed his eyes and paid his respects one last time. Tomorrow he would will himself to move on, to leave his pain and his tragedy behind. He would begin a new life with his new bride and finally walk away from the past.

He hoped.

The cry of crows in the distance and the occasional low of his neighbors' cattle were the only sounds that broke the silence. Brent gazed around at the bowing heads of seeded corn swaying to nature's rhythm in the wind blowing across the open field. The brilliant sunshine made him squint against its brightness. He closed his eyes and soaked it all in, allowing himself a final moment of heartache as he remembered the love he'd lost.

The moment was disturbed by Kip shrilly calling his name. "Mr. Taylor, sir! Where you been?"

Brent drew in a deep breath. "What are you doing here, Kip? I told you I was unavailable today. I asked you to take care of things for me and not come looking for me."

Kip stopped in his tracks, suddenly remembering his boss's request. "Aw shucks, I'm sorry, Mr. Taylor. I forgot all about it." Guilt washed over the young boy's face. "But one of the hens seems awful sick."

"You're more than capable of handling that yourself, Kip."

Kip hung his head. "I know, but…can't you just come take a look?"

Brent turned away, his jaw clenched. He didn't like to have to admonish Kip, and on any other day he would have been more than happy to help. But today was the last day he'd set aside to remember Annabelle and honor her memory. He was more than a bit anxious about meeting his new bride tomorrow, and needed the time to prepare himself, to be sure he was doing the right thing.

"Brent, is anything wrong?" Kip waited anxiously for an answer.

"Three years today, Kip. Three years today that Annabelle had her accident."

The boy's face turned ashen—Brent had told him and his father about that. "Sorry, Mr. Taylor. I didn't remember that neither."

Brent sighed. "It's alright, Kip. Come on—you'd better show me that hen."

The following morning, Brent awoke early after just a few hours' sleep. Even without dealing with that hen the day before, he would have had trouble sleeping. Today was the day he was meeting, and marrying, Christy Hancock of Philadelphia (by way of Topeka). Once again, he wondered what she would be like—and whether he was doing the right thing.

Everything within him shied away from marrying a woman he'd never met. But that was just the trouble—he'd never met another woman he wanted to marry. And out here, he never would. The only people he saw these days were his married neighbors and their children, the elderly folks and young families that attended the Baptist church on the outskirts of Newton, the men at the feed supply store, and the occasional Cherokee or Arapahoe family warily skirting the encroaching whites like himself. Single young women here were rarer than diamonds. It made sense for him to have a mail-order bride.

But the whole idea of it still made him so nervous, his stomach did flips as he dressed.

He pulled on his best shirt and tie, noticing for the first time how dingy they were in the light. He tried to rub a clean spot on the dusty mirror he'd cadged from his late mother's bedroom, but it didn't help the way he felt. His pants needed mending and his boots should have been cleaned long ago. Too late for that now. He had to hope she wouldn't mind how raggedy he looked.

He tramped outside to attach his wagon to Patty. The bay horse wasn't young anymore but was still a little flighty, with a sensitive mouth. He was strong, though, and a keen driving horse. He climbed into the wagon and waved goodbye to Kip. For the second day in a row he was trusting the farm to his young farmhand. "Take care," he called, then clucked Patty into a trot.

As he turned onto the main road and left the boundary of his property, Brent passed the field where the day before he'd gone to remember. Three years and one day. It was time to move on. And with God's help, he would do just that.

The Rock Island Line train arrived in Newton just after lunch, and Christy walked to the exit with shaky legs. For a moment her hand lingered on the door frame, a part of her wanting to stay inside the safety of the carriage. But then the whistle blew and the person behind Christy nudged her onto the platform.

Anxious, it took a few moments to get her footing as she strained to pick Brent out of the crowd. She knew to look for a man carrying a bunch of daisies, but she couldn't see anyone fitting that description. Her stomach was in knots—she was terrified that the man she was there to meet might be mean or even ugly. She knew she ought not to think such things, that she should want a man who was kind and responsible no matter what he looked like. But she couldn't quell her fears that she would be repulsed by him or forced to live with a man she couldn't abide.

But as she finally caught sight of Brent Taylor, she knew she had nothing to worry about. There he was at the end of the platform, a few wilted daisies in his hands and a look of curiosity on his face. She smiled at him and waved, and he returned the smile, tipping his hat.

She watched him stride toward her on the platform, averting her eyes every time he caught them. He's to be the first man I ever kiss...but will I love him? She gazed at his full lips, imagining what it would be like to press hers against them. Would they kiss at the wedding? She was still hoping for a romantic white wedding with all of the trimmings, but glancing around at the dusty town, she considered that a bit far-fetched.

She certainly couldn't have asked for a more handsome groom, though. His tanned features were accentuated by sparkling blue eyes, and his muscular physique wasn't hidden by the gray morning coat and pants, blue button-down shirt and...was that a silk cravat? She didn't expect her future husband to show up in such finery—but then, he wasn't a native to the West any more than she was. Apparently she had still been daydreaming of cowboys in leather chaps. But Brent Taylor was, from all appearances, a gentleman.

Christy's heart fluttered as he drew near, realizing that God really had provided for her—not just a husband, but one that would understand both her trials and her Eastern upbringing. Still, she wondered how she'd even speak to him, let alone kiss him. His eyes seemed to bore into her soul as though he could see and understand her every thought. She shivered with delight and nervousness.

Chapter Ten

Brent was taken aback by how lovely Christy Hancock was in person. The photo the agency had sent him right after they made the match didn't do justice to her shining red hair piled high in large curls on top of her head, nor her striking green eyes, nor her peaches-and-cream complexion, nor her curvaceous figure. He swallowed nervously as he dipped his hat and made his way to her, his legs trembling as he walked.

When he reached her side, he wanted more than anything to scoop her up into his arms and kiss her full red lips. He figured on settling for a polite peck on the cheek, but now that he was close enough to see the frightened look in her eyes, he realized with a sinking stomach that even that might be too much for her just yet.

Her jaw clenched and she coughed anxiously before she finally got the nerve to whisper a quiet "hello."

Brent reached out and took her shaking hand. "Miss Hancock," he said, trying to keep his voice as warm and welcoming as possible. "It's a pleasure to finally meet you. I have been looking forward to it." Miss Hancock nodded. It was clear to him she was having great difficulty. "I have somewhere for us to clean up before the ceremony. So we can look tidy."

Miss Hancock dropped her head, and Brent mentally kicked himself. Look tidy?!? No doubt she wanted to look more than "tidy" on her wedding day—she probably wanted to wear a long white gown trimmed in frilly, expensive lace. But she was going to have to make do with the clothes she was wearing. Not one minute in, and he'd already put his foot in his mouth.

Now to see if he could make up for it. "I think you look very pretty, Miss Hancock."

That seemed to help. "Thank you, Mr. Taylor. Um… you look very nice too."

"Thank you, ma'am." Okay, that was better. "Well, shall we?" He offered her his arm. She took it and they headed to his wagon. An enterprising porter had loaded her trunk and bags onto a cart, and followed behind.

Only once the wagon was loaded and the porter departed did she speak again. "What…what shall we be doing now?"

"Well, of course the first stop is the courthouse, to be married," Brent replied. "We'll need to get back to the farm before evening, since I left my farmhand Kip in charge for the day."

Miss Hancock nodded, and her face fell. Brent cringed, wondering how he'd blown it this time. Not arranging a church wedding? Not booking a night in town for their honeymoon? This was an Eastern lady, after all—she had expectations, and he hadn't even considered them. She probably never imagined her marriage would be conducted in such haste—just arrived in Newton and already being whisked away to her wedding ceremony. Brent, you fool! he scolded himself.

But she summoned her courage quickly. "All right," she said, if a little stiffly. "Let's go." And even if it wasn't enthusiastic, the sound of her voice cheered him.

Newton itself was a quaint hamlet, with the unfinished look one would expect from a boomtown a few months old. It was dusty and lined with raw timber storefronts and buildings. Wagons pulled by sturdy horses bounced up and down the streets and folks stood on street corners and in doorways chatting with their neighbors. The county courthouse was a squat wooden building, whitewashed to help it stand out. Brent helped Miss Hancock down and led her up the path to the front door.

But when they reached it, she took a step backward and almost tripped down the courthouse steps. She shook her head. "No," she murmured.

"What's the matter, Miss Hancock?" Brent asked, turning to look at her.

"Mr. Taylor...aren't we going to be married by a minister? At your church?"

He shook his head. "I'm afraid the preacher is out of town today. He's over at the Blacks' farm since Sarah Black just had her fifth baby and she's not faring well. So we need to make do with what we have."

"But it's important to me that we're married with a minster present."

"I'm sorry, ma'am. I did ask him, but as I said, he was called away."

"Can we wait—until he gets back to town?" Panic was creeping into her voice.

"I wish we could, ma'am, but I have to get back to

my farm. It doesn't run without me. And I can't take you back to the farm with me unless we're married, can I? Besides, there's really no place for us to stay in town—there's no hotel, just a working men's boarding house. Let's just get married today—it doesn't matter who does the marrying so long as it's done. Then we can head on home and take care of things there." He sounded a little panicked himself, come to think—as though he was afraid she'd run away. Maybe he was.

Miss Hancock stood outside the courthouse doors, stricken with indecision. She didn't seem to want to cause a fuss, but it was clear she was disappointed—and scared.

Brent's voice was pleading. "Please come inside, Miss Hancock. Judge Hanley will do fine by us, I promise. Even with only a judge, it will be a marriage as good as any in the eyes of God and the law."

Finally, she nodded. Unsure what else he could do, Brent opened the door and led her inside.

Judge Hanley was a balding, fat man with a rough manner and little patience. He frowned at them as he recited the vows for them to repeat. Soon they were done and he declared them man and wife in the eyes of God, with the court clerk as their witness. The ceremony was over in minutes.

After three years' delay, Brent was finally married. He smiled—until he looked at his downcast new bride. He knew he had to find a way to put a smile on her beautiful face.

Chapter Eleven

They walked down the courthouse stairs in silence, the distance between them seeming to grow with each step. Christy's eyes welled up and she had to turn away so that Mr. Taylor—Brent—wouldn't see her cry. This is nothing like how I imagined it would be, she thought. No guests, no flowers, no grand ceremony, no white dress, no lavish spread of food to share with family and friends. Not even a kiss.

And worst of all, no parents by her side. Despite her best efforts to conceal her tears, her chest began to heave.

"Miss, er, Christy?" Brent said, laying a gentle hand on her arm. "I know the ceremony wasn't everything you might have hoped for. I'm very sorry."

She straightened, shaking her head as she sobbed. "It's not that. I just miss Mam and Daddy terribly. I miss them every day, but most of all at a time like this..." She began to weep again.

But her new husband truly was a gentleman. He put his arms around her, stroking her hair as he let her cry. And when she finally stopped, he gave her a chaste squeeze and stepped back to look her in the eye. "What happened to them, and to you, was awful," he said gently. "No one should have to see their parents die like that. It's a horrible thing for anyone to live through. And I promise, I will do whatever I can to make your life a happy one, and help you heal from what happened."

For a moment, she couldn't speak. Finally she managed to choke out a "thank you."

Her new husband smiled and nodded. "Let's be getting home. You've had a long day—perhaps you'll feel better once you've had a rest."

Back in the wagon, though, Christy couldn't rest. She shifted uncomfortably on the rough seat as she tried to devise something to say to the stranger sitting beside her. Well, there was always the weather. "It's very warm out. Quite different from Philadelphia."

Brent nodded. "It's drier, though, I imagine."

"Yes, it is." *What have I gotten myself into?* She sat stiffly, her hands pressed tightly together in her lap.

"I apologize if I seem a bit tired," Brent said. "I had to stay up late last night. With a sick hen," he added with a chuckle.

"Is she better now?" she asked.

He nodded. "Thankfully, she seems to be. I'm more used to taking care of horses—I didn't think a hen would be so much work."

She snuck a glimpse at the man sitting next to her. *He did seem happy when he first saw me. He smiled at me, and it lit me all up inside. But now he's nervous. Huh. Maybe it's not just me—maybe we both have trouble getting used to this.* Strangely, that gave her hope. She wasn't alone in this.

Christy turned back to the road, and frowned as she saw something ahead of them. “What is that?”

Brent squinted at the horizon and shook his head. “I don’t see anything.”

“There!” Christy yelped. “Watch out!” A rattlesnake lay in the middle of the road, hissing and rattling its tail.

Patty reared up on his hind legs with a startled whinny. The wagon leaned precariously to one side, spilling Christy and Brent out onto the road. She caught the brunt of the impact. “Christy!” Brent called in dismay, rushing over to where she laid in the dirt.

“Where’s…the snake?” she asked breathlessly.

“Long gone, I’d say.” Brent tried to help her to her feet.

She pushed him away, still searching frantically for the snake. She’d never seen a creature like that in Pennsylvania. As she tried to stand, she realized her ankle was swollen and her left leg was bruised.

“Stay still, Christy—you’re hurt.”

“Why did the horse do that?” she asked, pushing Brent away more forcefully this time, and struggled to her feet despite the pain. She was furious. “Why didn’t you listen to me when I warned you about the snake?” she asked. “Didn’t you believe me?”

“I’m sorry, Christy—I just didn’t see it.” Brent went after the horse and grabbed him by the reins, pulling him to a halt and bringing him back. “Here—are you well enough to hold the reins while I check Patty and the wagon for damage and make sure that darn snake has skedaddled?”

Christy nodded and hobbled over to the horse with a scowl. She tried to hold the horse still while Brent checked the wheels of the wagon and looked around the roadside for the snake. "Whoa—easy, boy," she said as the horse turned his head and began to nibble her hair. "What's he doing that for?" she squealed.

Brent looked up. "He's just curious. Hold him still for a minute. I can't see the rattler anywhere, but I need to tighten one of the bolts holding this rear wheel in place. Almost done..."

She felt her heart beat faster as the horse brought his head close to hers again, his hot breath against her neck. The animal opened its mouth and bared yellowing teeth at her. She squealed and dropped the reins, jumping back in fright—and the horse bolted. She watched in wide-eyed dismay as he galloped off, taking the wagon with him and knocking Brent aside.

"Christy!" he called out. "Catch him!" But she was frozen to the spot in fright, and the horse was far too quick for her. He was a hundred yards down the road before she could process what had happened.

Brent stood and brushed himself off, his face dark as thunder. "How could you let that happen? Now we'll have to walk and who knows what will happen to Patty. He might hurt himself and he's a valuable beast. What were you thinking?"

Christy turned on him, her red curls coated in dust and dirt and laying limp around her face. "Me? This is hardly my fault—I've never handled a horse on my own before and I was doing my best! That creature was trying to eat my hair!" She reached a shaking hand up to her messy locks.

Brent looked at her, then burst into laughter, as if the whole situation were hilarious. She grew even angrier watching him. He was laughing at her, making fun of her when she was hurt, tired and dirty. She'd never felt more alone in her life.

He noticed her glower and calmed down, finishing with a small cough. "He was…he wasn't going to eat the hair off your head, Christy," he told her, a little embarrassed.

She crossed her arms and pouted. "Well, how was I to know? I think you're being awfully rude to me, Mr. Taylor! I'm all alone with a strange man in the middle of nowhere, and you blame me because your horse isn't properly trained?"

He sighed. "It's not so difficult to hold onto a horse's reins. I thought you would know how. I just hope I haven't lost a valuable horse and wagon because you didn't!" Now he was glaring at her.

She felt her lips trembling again. "I wish I'd never come to this awful place," she whispered. "It was a mistake. Why did I think I could find any kind of happiness marrying a stranger?" Then she noticed the stung look on Brent's face and wanted to bite her tongue. She wished she could take the words back.

"Well," he said, turning away, "that makes two of us then, I suppose."

Christy swallowed. She'd come all this way, only to be so rude she'd turned her own groom away. If he'd wanted her before, he certainly didn't now. And now it was too late—they'd already gotten married. It was all just one terrible mistake.

"We need to find Patty and the wagon," Brent said tersely and strode down the road.

She followed after him, tears streaming down her dirty cheeks. "Brent, I'm sorry! I…" But he didn't even look back, let alone reply.

They walked in silence for more than two miles, Christy bravely attempting to hide her limp as she gingerly shifted her weight off of her injured ankle. Brent strode down one side of the road, while she hobbled as quickly as she could along the other. She kept trying to sneak glances at Brent without him noticing. Every time he looked her way, she felt tingles run up and down her body, even as the shame hit her all over again.

Why had she spouted off, telling him she regretted coming here? She recalled the look on his face as she'd said it, and it sent a dagger through her heart every time. Did he mean what he said? Does he wish I'd never come? Can I blame him? After the way I acted, I wouldn't be surprised if he wants nothing more to do with me. Maybe it's for the best—I don't belong here. How could I ever hope to make a life here when I can't even keep hold of a horse? How could I possibly think I could be his partner in life and help him to run a farm?

Guilt plagued her as she prayed they would find the wagon and the horse in one piece. I don't care about my possessions, God. But please let the horse and wagon be found, so Brent doesn't suffer any more loss. And let him forgive me for the harsh words I said to him.

She stopped suddenly and shielded her eyes from the sun. "Look!" she cried, pointing ahead of them on the winding track.

"What is it?" Brent snapped. "Another snake?"

"No." Christy hurried down the road as best she could. "My trunk!" She limped to the luggage, only to find the lid broken and all her clothing, even those donated to her by Meredith, strewn far and wide in the dirt. "Oh dear. I suppose it's just as I deserve," she murmured.

Brent walked over to join her. "Don't worry. We'll find everything and see what we can do about fixing your trunk. And…well, at least we know he went this way."

Christy nodded. "I feel bad because some of these things were given to me by Meredith—Mrs. Poke, the woman I stayed with in Topeka. She probably trusted me to take better care of them than this." She hung her head.

Brent reached out his hand and placed it gingerly on her arm. She looked and saw a faint flush creep up his neck. "I've been thinking…and I'm sorry. It wasn't all your fault. I should have realized you'd be scared and nervous on your first day here. And I should've asked what you can handle, rather than assuming. I apologize for yelling at you, and for not being more understanding."

Christy stared at her broken trunk. "I forgive you. And…can you forgive me for saying I wish I hadn't come? I feel so helpless, so worthless. And I feel like I've let Meredith and my Mam down. If they could see me right now they'd be ashamed of my childish behavior, I just know it."

He offered a half-smile, and her arm warmed and tingled under his hand. "Of course I forgive you. And I'm sure they wouldn't be ashamed, Christy. You're doing your best and you've been very brave. It just takes time to adjust, is all."

"Thank you," she squeaked. It was all she could manage.

He turned his head to look at the sun high over her shoulder. "I'm wondering if we'll make it back before sundown. I…if you really don't feel you belong here,

I won't keep you here against your will. I'll take you back to the train station the day after tomorrow if that's what you want. But for now, we have to get moving—it's getting late."

Christy followed his gaze, admiring the colorful hues that the setting sun threw across the wide sky. She looked down at his hand, still resting on her arm. His touch was softer than she'd imagined it would be. *But if this isn't where I belong, even his touch making me feel alive inside for the first time in a long time can't change that. Was I only fooling myself to think that this scheme could ever work out?*

She pulled her arm from his grasp. "We'd best find your horse and wagon, then." For the other concern, she didn't have a solution.

"There's the wagon," said Brent.

Christy and he were walking side-by-side along the track, having repacked and closed her trunk where it landed. She looked up and sighed in relief. Even better, Patty the horse was standing by the roadside grazing, his reins dragging on the ground.

"Tired himself out and stopped for lunch, by the looks of it," he commented as they reached the bay. He patted him down and checked him for injuries.

Christy was tired as well, but didn't have the option of grazing. She straightened up the back of the wagon—thankfully, her other luggage had stayed in the bed.

Brent guided Patty over to the wagon and backed him into the shafts. "Looks like his collar is fine and the traces don't appear to be broken, only torn here where the buckle was attached. I think I can make it work using a different buckle hole." He squatted down to fix it. "There, that should get us home after we go back for your trunk. He's had enough rest that we can ride—if he hasn't scared you off it."

Christy climbed down from the back of the wagon, walked over to the horse and patted him gently on the neck. "I'll take the chance—I'm too tired to walk all the way. At least we know now we'll make it back before sundown."

Brent smiled at her. "If you're sure."

She returned the smile. "Yes, I'm sure." About that day, anyway.

Chapter Twelve

"We're home," said Brent, pointing to the ranch house on a rise overlooking the fields in front of them. "It's not much, I suppose..."

"It's lovely," Christy responded. She'd been afraid to say it, but part of her had been worried she'd be coming to a log cabin, or one of the sod houses she'd seen on the train trip there. But Brent's home was a beautiful structure with a solid shingled roof and a wide verandah that flowed around the outside of the building. The structure was painted a brilliant white that stood out against the greens and yellows of the grasses. Several good-sized glass windows along the front of the house overlooked a vegetable garden, and a dusty wagon track circled from the house to the solid square doors of a tall timber barn.

She was exhausted, but the sight of it filled her with delight. She opened her eyes wide as she took in the sprawling building. "Wow, you've got room for a large family and more! I can see why you were lonely, living all alone in such a big place—" She stopped talking and blushed. It seemed uncouth to her to reference the admissions he'd made in his letters, now that they weren't sure if the union was a mistake.

But he smiled widely at her. So maybe she was worrying too much.

Brent stopped Patty in front of the house, undid the traces and led the horse into the barn to rub him down. Christy followed behind, observing quietly. Once Patty was dry, Brent locked him in a stall and threw in a bale of hay. The horse dropped his head and took a bite, munching happily, his ears flicking back and forth.

Next, Brent led Christy back to the house and up the front path. "Now, I should warn you, it's not all it could be. I'm not much at housekeeping, and the crops keep me busy outdoors, so..." He pushed the front door open and guided her inside.

She didn't think much of the warning at first. The house looked so lovely from the outside that she had little concern about the interior. But the inside of the farmhouse was another thing entirely. The first room was an open living area with two large chairs before the hearth and a sturdy dining table with two more chairs. The kitchen lay beyond, hosting a stout cast-iron stove with a pipe leading up to and through the high ceiling. A brick oven dominated one wall and a sturdy worktable sat under a square window.

However, every room was full of dust, cobwebs, dirt and chaos, each in a worse state of disarray than the one before it. Christy wandered through them in dismay. Down a wide hallway, she found four separate bedrooms. Two were empty, and a third was full of unpacked boxes and furniture, including a few bookshelves. At the end of the hall, the master bedroom held a large feather bed, two bureaus, a trunk and…no, that wasn't a dead rat, just a sock.

Brent caught Christy's expression of horror. "I'm sure it will clean up just fine," he said, not sounding sure at all.

She forced a smile. "Of course it will. It's safe and dry, and that's all I can ask for."

He looked relieved as he hurried to put her trunk and bags in the bedroom. Then they returned to the living room to stand in awkward silence, looking at each other. Her stomach flipped, once. *Maybe I could stay here after all…if he wants me to.*

He stared hard at the fireplace and cleared his throat. "Well, you're all set in the bedroom. I'll sleep on the floor out here—I just need to get a fire going."

"Oh," she said. That confirmed that he was no more sure than she was. "Okay, then. Thank you."

"There's a bit of bread and cheese in the kitchen if you're hungry," he offered.

"Thank you," she said, suddenly feeling ravenous. She went in, took a piece of bread from the breadbox and sat on a chair at the dining table to eat it. He did the same and quickly sat down opposite her, removing his hat and placing it on the table beside him. She smiled at him and bit into the crusty bread, savoring the yeasty flavor.

After their "meal," Christy retired to the bedroom. She didn't even unpack her bags, in case Brent decided to take her back to the train station and say goodbye to her forever. She hugged herself and stared out through the bedroom window across the darkening farm. The sun had dipped past the horizon and a chill breeze blew over the waving fields of grass. Her throat tightened as she thought about leaving this place. I've only just arrived—has it already won my heart?

Christy prepared for bed and lay down on the comfortable mattress. It had been a day full of surprises and she had survived them all. She wondered what the next day would bring.

The following day, Brent was up bright and early to tend to his farm.

"Oh dear, I must have slept for hours!" Christy muttered, chiding herself when she awoke and saw the sun high in the sky. She washed up, using a small jug of water and a cloth that sat on a bedside table in her room. Feeling refreshed, she wandered out to the kitchen to find something for breakfast, and discovered a hard-boiled egg Brent had left on the kitchen table, with a note beside it that read, "Good morning!"

She smiled and cracked open the egg, biting into it with relish. She felt guilty about sleeping so late when Brent had obviously gone straight to work, but she was tired after a long journey. Her whole body ached from being flung from the wagon and then having to walk to find it. And her ankle throbbed when she put weight on her left foot.

Still, though she might be returning to Topeka the next day, she didn't want Brent to think her lazy. She gazed around the dusty and disorganized farmhouse. In the bright light of day it didn't seem as bad as it had the previous evening.

She peeked out the back door, wondering where he might be. He wasn't anywhere to be seen, but she did notice her trunk sitting there—he had mended it and wiped it clean. He'd also given the clothing in it a cursory wash and hung it out to dry on a line. Christy's eyes filled with tears and her throat ached. She couldn't believe he'd done all that. It was so kind, so considerate.

After the way she'd spoken to him yesterday, she was surprised he was willing to do anything at all for her. She'd behaved like a spoiled child. But here he was, taking care of her before she'd even rolled out of bed. A gentleman, yes.

Christy ventured outside and gazed around the property. It sparkled and gleamed in the morning light, and she drew in a deep breath of the fresh, sweetly-scented air. It felt good to be outside. She strolled down the path toward the barn and let the sun warm her face. Hands pushed high above her head, she stretched and smiled. They'd gotten off to a rocky start, but the land certainly was lovely. It had a homey feel to it, as though welcoming her with open arms. The appeal of adventure was too much for her, and she set off to explore the property. She picked a few wildflowers along the way, sticking them behind her ears and in her hair.

As she skipped down a trail, she stumbled over a rock and fell, landing on her outstretched hands. She felt them splat into something warm and sticky. "What on earth?" She lifted her hands to her face and sniffed them.

"Augh! Manure!" She crawled from the path to a tuft of long grasses, where she scrubbed her hands vigorously to rid them of the dung. She scrunched up her nose and stood to her feet.

As she peered around, wondering which way she should go next, she heard a short bark near her feet. She jumped backward, landing on her rear. A large rodent stood close by, its hackles raised. It barked again before darting into a hole in the ground, sending her scuttling backward like a crab. The next thing she knew, she was rolling down an embankment, landing with a splash in a reedy creek bed.

The cold water seeped through her clothing in a moment, and she gasped. This adventure was not going well. And what was that creature? It looked like a big squirrel. What other wild animals could she expect to stumble across out here? Perhaps she should head back to the house.

She heaved herself up from the creek bed, the weight of the water dragging at her full skirts. Stumbling forward, she climbed up the bank to the level field. With a few swipes of her hands, she did her best to wipe the mud and sticks from her gown, but stared in dismay at her sodden leather boots. Oh well, it couldn't be helped. She'd just have to dry them out, oil and polish them the first chance she got. Hopefully Brent had some leather oil and shoe polish on hand.

Limping along in her wet boots, Christy made her way back. The sun was high in the sky now and she'd lost track of time. It had to be near lunchtime, and she really should prepare something to take to Brent. He was working somewhere on the property, no doubt wondering why he'd ever considered marriage.

She hurried into the yard and was walking up the front steps when Brent emerged from the house, almost running her over. "Excuse me," he said, placing his hands against her shoulders. He noted her disheveled appearance and suppressed a smirk. "What on Earth happened to you?"

"Well… I went for a walk, fell in manure, some kind of big rat barked at me and I fell into a creek."

He chuckled. It lit up his face and brought a sparkle to his blue eyes. “A rat? Maybe a prairie dog. They’re not usually aggressive, though. Are you okay?”

“Well, I suppose, but it did give me a fright. Otherwise I’m fine, just a bit wet and dirty. Thank you for fixing my trunk, and for washing my clothes. You really didn’t have to do all of that. It was very kind.”

“I don’t mind. It was my fault, after all. I should never have asked you to hold Patty.”

“No, it wasn’t your fault at all, it was mine. But thank you.”

Brent’s nose wrinkled. “I don’t mean to be rude, but…”

“Oh yes—the manure.” Christy sniffed her hands and drew back in disgust. “I tried to wipe them clean, but I suppose I need a bath.”

Brent laughed and pulled his hat from his head. “I’ll draw a bath for you. While you’re waiting, why don’t you check out the chicken coop in back?” He strode back into the house.

Christy shoved her soiled hands behind her back and wandered from the verandah around the outside of the house. The garden in front was large, but overgrown. Tomato bushes ran wild alongside a massive pumpkin vine and an assortment of herbs, vegetables and gargantuan weeds. She shook her head in dismay—it would take a lot of work to get it back into order.

Behind the house stood a well-maintained chicken coop full of plump brown-and-black-feathered chickens. They strutted around the coop clucking and crooning, pecking at the ground and scratching with their long claws. A rooster perched on a branch that angled across the top of the coop on one side, its ends poking out through the wire fencing. His bright plumage stood out against the plain colors of the hens.

She pulled the door of the coop open, crouched down and crept through. A feathery smell overpowered the scent of her hands, which was a mercy. She picked her way through the coop, careful where her feet fell. A large timber box, accessible through a hatch door, held the nests.

Lifting the door, she reached inside, finding several warm eggs that she squirreled into her skirt pockets. But as her fingers discovered another egg, a hair-raising squawk came from within the nesting box and she found her hand under attack. A hen flew at her, pecking and scratching with fury. She pulled back with a scream and stumbled from the coop. With a bang, she slammed the door closed behind her and stood panting outside. Her hand was scratched, and she even saw a little blood on one finger.

Farm life was more challenging than she'd realized. If she even had the chance to stick with it.

Chapter Thirteen

"Bath's ready!" Brent called from inside the house.

Christy sighed with relief and hobbled to the back door. Brent met her there with a towel to dry her feet. She set the eggs in a bowl on the kitchen worktable, wrapped herself in the towel and followed him to the bedroom, where a large claw-footed tub sat behind a white folding screen. She blushed, not realizing before that it was there. The bed was now neatly made, and a rocking chair had been brought in, with another towel sitting on it. It's like he thinks of everything, she thought.

"Feel free to get what you need from your bags," he told her. "I'll be outside working, so don't slip in the tub." He chuckled again and left the room.

She could hear him whistling as he headed for the barn, and felt her cheeks warm. There was something very attractive about Brent Taylor. The way he laughed so playfully at her, then took care of her without a second thought. How he whistled as he went about his work, as if he didn't have a care in the world. She smiled, remembering the look on his face when she'd told him about the prairie dog.

She collected the clothing she needed and returned to the bath, where she noticed Brent had thoughtfully provided a cake of soap and a washcloth. He'd even set a foot towel beside the tub to keep her from slipping on the floorboards when she was done.

She undressed and slipped into the warm water, exhaling as it enveloped her tired body. It'd been so long since she'd had a bath like this—since leaving Philadelphia, she'd had to wash in small basins and bowls. It was such a relief to be able to sink into a full tub. The warmth soaked into her bones, and she felt a renewed sense of peace.

When she emerged from the tub, she smelled of soap and the lavender sachets she always stored with her clothing. With a fresh work dress (courtesy of the Pokes) and wet hair, she felt like a new person. She smiled, strolled out to the kitchen—and was reminded with a look around how much work the house needed. Between that and the garden, it could keep her busy for months if she stayed.

She frowned and rolled up her sleeves. "Hmm… where should I start?"

Well, right there was as good a place as any. She found an old apron stashed in a drawer under the kitchen table, wrapped it around her dress and tied it behind her back. With some rummaging, she found everything she needed to bake bread and began mixing and kneading. Before long, she had a long loaf of dough in a pan, ready to rise.

She stepped out the back door and set the covered pan in the sunshine, then gazed around. There were so many brilliant colors in the fields, with flowers blooming everywhere. She gathered as many wildflowers as her arms could hold, brought them into the house and went back for a second load. Cadging some glasses and tall bowls, she turned them into makeshift vases and made sure each room of the house was filled with the sweet scent of wild flowers. "Now, that's more like it."

Next, she found some flour sacks and a broom and began dusting away all the dirt and cobwebs, wiping every surface in the house clean. She opened every window that would, and let the fresh breezes blow in the scent of warm grasses. The whole house took on a different character. She allowed herself a moment to admire her handiwork. *It looks so lovely now.*

But there was still the possibility she'd have to leave the next day. And then what would she do? Where would she go?

Christy sat down at the dining table, letting the tears fall. She knew she was capable of taking care of herself once the inheritance left her by her parents was finally settled. She could make her way to California and study for her teaching certificate, or go back East. But even though she knew she could, she felt more miserable the more she thought about it.

She wasn't sure why, but there was something about this place that made her want to stay and put down roots. Something about the beautiful countryside and the charming farmhouse—and the gentleman who owned it—seemed like home to her. Even though it had been in such disarray when she first entered it a day ago, she was already imagining spending evenings knitting or reading in front of the hearth, side by side with Brent.

She could picture herself cooking meals in the

kitchen for their growing family, surrounded by the laughter and shouts of children that would fill the spacious homestead. She'd begun to believe she never would again feel at home after losing her parents—and yet here in Indian Territory she'd discovered a place she felt inextricably at peace. She stared out the window at the swaying grasses and clucking hens and sighed. It was a beautiful place.

She shook her head and took a deep breath. There was no point picturing a future for herself there—not until it was clear she'd be able to stay. Brent could toss her on the train to Topeka tomorrow, so she had to consider what her life might look like elsewhere. Maybe teaching would become a passion for her—she certainly enjoyed the company of children. And she'd heard that California was a beautiful and wonderfully adventurous place.

Time to put the bread in the oven. She hurried outside and lifted the cloth from the pan. The bread had risen beautifully, its puffy white dough smelled like yeast and sunshine. She carried it carefully into the house and slid it into the pre-warmed brick oven. At least she'd have this memory to take with her, should she have to leave.

Just after noon, Christy walked out to the front porch to beat the dust out of the living room rug, and saw Brent coming up over the hill with a tall, wiry boy, driving a pair of oxen in front of them. They guided them into the corral by the barn and began bringing out hay for them. She stood very still as she watched Brent and the boy work. The sun beat down hard on them—she could see why their skin was so suntanned.

It must be hard work, running this ranch. If I stayed here, would I be able to help him?

Suddenly her mind raced as she imagined the life they could live together—Brent rearing and branding cattle and horses, while she decorated the house, making it the perfect sanctuary for him to come home to every night. She sighed again loudly and strode back into the house to return the rug to its place on the floor.

Checking the bread, she looked out the back door and spotted something she hadn't noticed before: a large lemon tree. Several bright yellow fruits hung from its branches among a myriad of green. She went out, pulled the ripened ones she could reach from the branches and placed them in her apron. She found a basket by the back door—I wish I'd seen that this morning for the eggs, she thought fleetingly—dropped them into it and carried it to the kitchen worktable.

A further search of the kitchen unearthed some cured ham hanging in the larder, and scavenging through the overgrown garden yielded a basket of freshly plucked tomatoes and cucumbers. The bread was done, so she set it out to cool and began preparing sandwiches and lemonade. Filling the basket with the food and a blanket, she carried it out the door to the barn where Brent and the boy were working.

Brent looked up as she walked toward him. He caught her eyes and smiled tenderly at her. "What have you got there?" he asked.

"I thought you might be hungry," said Christy, shading her eyes with one hand while she held up the picnic basket in the other.

Brent nodded toward a shady spot under a large oak tree beside the barn. "We sure are! Why don't the three of us picnic over there?"

She smiled shyly and nodded. Under the oak, she set

the basket down and pulled the blanket out to spread across the grass and leaves. The two men washed up at the water pump and walked over to join her.

"Christy, this is Kip Harris. He helps around the place and lives over yonder with his parents," Brent pointed down the road toward Newton.

"Pleased to meet you, Kip." She smiled at him and handed him a sandwich.

Kip took the sandwich with a nod. "Ma'am," he said and gulped the whole thing down in just a few bites.

Christy looked over at Brent and giggled at the sight of Kip's feeding frenzy. Brent returned the grin and they each munched on their sandwiches, sneaking glances at each other.

Chapter Fourteen

Brent had spent that morning in a temper. He'd snapped at Kip and yelled at the cows, and Patty bore the brunt of his frustration—he was spurred forward, then jerked to turn or stop. Kip watched him with a worried expression but didn't say anything.

Brent knew that there was a good chance Christy would want to hop the train to Topeka the following day, and he felt powerless to do anything about it. She was so beautiful that he almost became tongue-tied when he was around her. His heart would beat rapidly and his face grow flushed and his words come out all wrong. It seemed everything he said upset her one way or another.

It was all turning out wrong. He'd been so happy to stand beside her at the courthouse and marry her, imagining how their life might be when they returned to the farmhouse. But the ride home had gone awry due to that stupid snake, and since then everything had gone from bad to worse.

And then she emerged from the house with a packed lunch for them, and he felt a tremble course through his body. They sat close together on a blanket under the shade of a majestic tree, her with her legs curled up beneath her. A breeze blew a strand of curls against her white neck, and he could think of nothing other than kissing her skin there. He admired her rounded figure, how stunning she looked with the sun shining down on her, the way it seemed to pick up the golden highlights streaking through her red mane. *She looks lovely.*

And soon she might be lost to him forever. How unfair was that?

"I assume the hen is doing much better," she commented.

That stirred him from his musings. "Sorry, what?"

"The hen. When I collected eggs this morning, I couldn't tell that any of them had been ill. They were all walking around the coop as though they'd never been sick at all."

He nodded and swallowed the last of his sandwich. "She's good as new today, not that I can really take the credit. Later on, maybe I can point out which one it was."

Christy smiled shyly and set her sandwich down. "I'm sure you're very good to your animals, Brent. I was watching you from the window..." She stopped short.

"Y-you were?"

Christy blushed. "I mean, I was watching you with the two cows—just for a few moments. But I saw how gentle you were with them, making sure they were comfortable."

He nodded and grinned. "Thank you." He felt his neck beginning to flush red and feared that it would travel to his face, giving away his true feelings for her. He coughed into his hand and gazed across the field in front of them.

She took a last sip from her glass of lemonade, then stood up. “I’d better take these dishes back to the house.” She gathered the empty items into the basket and turned to leave. “I’ll see you back there for supper. If you like.”

He raised his eyebrows. “You’re going to cook?”

Christy smiled. “Yes. If that’s all right with you.”

He grinned, stars in his eyes. “I’ll be looking forward to it the rest of the day.”

She returned his smile with a look of relief, then walked back to the house. Brent watched her skirts sashaying as she moved across the lawn and wondered what he could possibly do before tomorrow to convince her to stay. He’d only known her for a day, but he didn’t want her to leave, not yet. Not before he had a chance to get to know her. He lifted his hat from his head and scratched, thinking on the matter, then shrugged and spun on his heel to return to work.

He saw Kip watching him with a sly grin. Oh well, it couldn’t be helped. Brent shook his head and he whistled as he walked back to the fields.

Christy was daydreaming as she stirred the stew on the stovetop, her mind returning to the thought of Brent’s lips. If only we could share a kiss before I leave. I wonder what it would be like. She imagined the firmness of his arms around her, pulling her close to his thick chest. Mam would have scolded her for such thinking. She shook her head and tried to ponder something else, but she couldn’t help it. She could not think clearly with him around.

It was for the best if she was to leave the next day. She didn’t know how she’d get anything at all done if she were to live with the man. She'd spend all her time woolgathering about his muscled arms and never get a moment's peace. It would be torturous.

A bubbling sound broke through her reverie, and she saw the stew was about to burn. She took it off the stove quickly and tasted it, praying it wasn't ruined. It was fine, and she breathed a sigh of relief. The last thing she wanted to do was to ruin the one supper she might ever make for Brent. If only there could be more. *Here I am just getting settled in, and to say goodbye already…*

Christy gazed out the window over the sweeping property and wished for a chance to make a home here. Already, she loved the lemon tree by the back door, the wide verandah around the house, the useful little kitchen, the hens clucking nearby. But most of all, she loved to see the smile on Brent's face as he watched her. And she loved watching him at that moment, the curve of his muscular arms as he swung an axe to split the firewood they needed for the evening's fire.

I have no home anywhere—that's likely the reason I find this place so inviting. I must remember to keep my wits about me. Brent doesn't want me here, and I don't belong. Mam would tell me to get my head out of the clouds and stop wishing for things that are never going to happen. I'll be back on the train tomorrow, and that's that.

When Brent finally tramped in the door that night, he was met with more than one surprise. First of all, he was taken aback by how pleasing the house looked. It wasn't sparkling clean, but most of the dust and cobwebs were gone and there were fresh flowers in every room. Then came the savory scent of the ham stew

Christy had prepared. He was hungry after a hard day's work on the ranch, and that warm, comforting aroma drew Brent to the table.

Christy served him an extra-large helping before they sat down to say the blessing together. She bowed her head and closed her eyes, and he took a moment to drink in the slope of her neck and the curve of her full lips before he closed his eyes to pray. After the blessing he took a bite as she watched expectantly. "It's delicious. I have to admit, I'm surprised to find you can cook so well."

Christy tasted it too. "I was taught to cook by my Mam. Did you really think she would let me grow up without knowing how to make a satisfactory meal?"

He shook his head so quickly he almost choked. "Gosh no, Christy—I meant no offense to your mother."

"I know," Christy replied. "It's okay. It's just that I miss her a lot."

"I understand. And I only meant…this is tastier than anything I've had in a long while." He smiled at her across the table. "Please take it as a compliment."

"I will. Thank you." She ducked her head shyly.

Brent continued eating the stew, marveling as the succulent flavors traveled over his tongue and warmed his stomach. He gazed across the table at Christy, watching as she took a bite. I misjudged her terribly yesterday. She's a kind woman with a sweet heart, not vain or silly at all.

He looked at the soft glossy curls piled high on her head. No longer streaked with dirt or dust, she'd tucked them up in a stylish manner that flattered her face and made her green eyes seem almost to glow in the firelight. She'd be the belle of any Louisville ball. A woman as beautiful as she is doesn't belong out here. It's for the best she wants to go back to the city.

Christy finished her bowl and stood to her feet. "I'll clean up now."

"You don't need to leave just yet. Sit with me a while. Besides," he added, his gaze sweeping around the house. "You've done more than enough cleaning and tidying for the day—I can see that."

She blushed. "I wasn't even sure you'd noticed."

"Of course I noticed. Why, the place is hardly recognizable as the same house I left this morning. You've done a wonderful job. It feels like…a real home."

She twisted her hands together. "I think it just needed a woman's touch."

Brent nodded and scooped the last bit of stew out of his bowl. "You're right about that. It reminds me now of my family home in Kentucky." He stopped eating and stared down into his bowl. It had been hard for him to lose his parents as well and he missed them the way Christy missed hers.

"I'm sure they were wonderful people."

"They were." His voice thickened as the memories washed over him.

Christy nodded, then took the plates to the kitchen in silence.

He cleared his throat and stood as well. "I…suppose we both ought to get some sleep. We've got another big journey ahead of us tomorrow."

She nodded and turned away. "Yes, we do."

Chapter Fifteen

As she washed the dishes and wiped the table clean, Christy could hear Brent arranging his bedding on the living room floor again. She paused, holding the dish-cloth in midair, as she listened to him bustle around. The possibility of a first kiss was getting more remote with each passing moment. Tomorrow they would make the journey back to the train station where they would separate forever. Her throat constricted with emotion and she focused her attention on scrubbing a stubborn piece of food from one of the plates.

When she finished cleaning up she crept quietly into the living room, dark now apart from the light of the candle in her hand. Brent was already lying on the floor. She stood and watched him for a moment, wondering if he was sleeping.

"Good night, Christy."

She was startled by the sound of his voice in the darkness. "Good night, Brent," she whispered and hurried to her room.

In bed, she read over Mam's letter, still able to hear her voice. Mam had written it months earlier, when

Christy went away over the summer with a friend. She'd read it then with tears in her eyes, and kept it close ever since.

The letter talked of the hopes and dreams her mother had for her, things she'd never been able to say in person poured out over several pages of sloped handwriting. She expressed her desire for Christy to grow into a strong, resilient woman, to find a good man to marry and to stick by him when times were tough. Most of all, she wanted Christy to learn to be happy and grateful for the things she had, rather than always wishing for more. She finished by telling her how much she loved her and was proud of everything she'd accomplished in her short life so far.

Christy hugged the letter to her chest. I wish I'd listened more to her while I had the chance. I wish I'd told her how I felt about her, her and Daddy. I took for granted that they'd always be here with me. And now they're gone.

She thought about all the times she'd grumbled when her mother pushed her forward and coaxed the best from her. Now all she wanted was to hear Mam's voice once more. She read the letter again, and again, wishing she didn't have to wake up the following day and face an unknown and lonely future. A future without her parents, without Brent and with no place to call home.

She lay down on the feather tick with the letter still in her hands and squeezed her eyes shut. How could she sleep, knowing what was taking place the next day? How could she wake up and walk out of this house that had already become home to her in such a short time? How could she face it?

A tear trickled down her cheek. It seems like all I've

done these last few months is say goodbye to people I love: Mam and Daddy, then the Pokes, now…

Christy stopped crying. She sniffled and stared into the candle flame. Do I love Brent? She picked up the old stuffed bear which she had laid on her pillow and held it to her chest. Surely, it can't be love. I've only known him for two days. Her heart ached at the thought of leaving him, that much was true. But she wasn't sure whether that was because she was heaping grief on top of more grief, or she was just scared of being alone, or whether she felt genuine love for the man.

I can't stay just because I'm scared or don't want to be alone. Loneliness had never been a problem for her—she made friends easily enough. But friends didn't replace a lost family. And family was what she longed for.

I will be all right by myself. I can survive. I can find a way to make it on my own…

But, she realized, she didn't want to survive alone. She didn't want to live without Brent, without a family. And it didn't have anything to do with her being scared. She just didn't want to go. She didn't want to leave the man she was falling in love with, who made her feel as though he could be her family.

But this just made matters all the worse. Now she could no longer comfort herself with the idea that it was only fear keeping her awake. Now she knew it was sadness, a pure, awful sorrow that had overtaken her whole body. She didn't want to leave. She began to weep, and cried and cried until there were no more tears and nothing for her exhausted body left to do but sleep.

She'd set the candle on the bedside table, and it burned brightly beside her bed. A breeze from the window fanned it higher, pushing the tip of the flame toward the edge of the letter in her motionless hand. And she'd fallen into so deep a sleep that nothing could wake her. The flame touched the edge of the paper, and her mother's words began to blacken. Within moments, the flame caught the bedding.

And still Christy slept, oblivious to the impending danger.

Brent was having trouble sleeping on the living room floor. He tossed and turned as he tried to get comfortable. Finally, he pushed the blanket back and gave up. "I'll be glad when she's gone and I get my bed back," he grumbled.

But even as he said it, he knew he didn't mean it. And he knew that his restlessness had nothing to do with the hard floor and everything to do with not wanting to send Christy away in the morning. He sighed, stood to his feet and stretched his arms high over his head, then headed outside for some fresh air.

He crept out the front door and pulled it shut silently behind him, careful not to wake Christy. Standing on the verandah, he leaned against the railing to gaze at the moon. This was supposed to be my second chance. I prayed for it, and God sent me a good, sweet woman—but all I've done is push her away. He felt ashamed of himself as he stood there. Please, God, I know I've already had more than my share of blessings, but please give me one last opportunity to make things right with Christy…

He paused mid-thought. Did he smell something burning?

He walked down the steps of the farmhouse and noticed a light in the bedroom window…too much light. For a moment he stood still, dumbstruck. Then he sprinted back into the house, scolding himself for leaving Christy alone.

He raced into the bedroom, where smoke almost overwhelmed him. Covering his mouth with his neckerchief, he ran to Christy, who still lay sleeping in the now-smoldering bed. He picked her up, carried her over his shoulder from the house and laid her down in the grass. “Wait here, my darling,” he said before racing back inside. Grabbing his blanket from the living room floor, he ran back to the bedroom and began beating at the flames.

Thankfully, the blaze itself wasn’t large, and he soon smothered it with the fabric. He coughed as he opened the window to let the smoke escape, then double-checked to see if any embers were still burning. Only after a few minutes could he survey the damage, but mercifully it was limited to the bed linens, a few papers and one slightly charred end table. No real harm done. He prayed a quick prayer of thanks to God for allowing him to be awake and to get to the fire before it was too late.

Remembering Christy, he hurried back to where she was still stretched out, lifeless in the grass. “Oh no…please, God, no.” He dropped to his knees beside her unmoving body and cried her name, rocking her body gently. When there was still no response he shook her, yelling for her to wake up. “Christy! Oh Christy, I should never have left you alone…” He pulled her close and held her tightly in his arms.

Only then did he feel it—her heartbeat. It was fine and strong, and she was breathing without difficulty.

He cupped a hand to stroke her cheek. "Please, my darling, wake up."

Christy's eyes sprang open and she gazed at Brent, wondering at his troubled face. She smiled at him. "Brent, whatever is the matter?" Then, confused, she rubbed her eyes and looked around. "And what on Earth are we doing out here?"

"Don't worry, Christy, you're all right now."

She looked down and saw the ash on her hand and the sleeve of her nightgown. She turned her head in alarm to look at the house. "Oh no!"

"The house is fine, Christy. There was a fire in the bedroom. You were unconscious." His voice almost broke as he told her what had happened. "Christy… I was so scared I was going to lose you."

She reached up her hand to touch his cheek, tracing the strong outline of his jawbone. He could feel her breath, warm against his face, and his heart pounded in his chest.

"Christy, do you think you could ever love me?" he whispered urgently, gazing down at her plump lips.

Christy's eyes filled with tears. Then, to his delighted surprise, she pulled his head toward her, her lips seeking his.

Chapter Sixteen

Christy couldn't believe she'd done that—initiated her first kiss. But you couldn't beat the setting—outside on the grass under a starry sky, Brent was cradling her in his strong arms. His lips were warm and soft, pulling gently at hers, returning her kiss with growing urgency. The tingling started at her mouth and spread all the way to her toes. She heard him moan softly as he held her tight in his embrace.

After a few moments, they each pulled away, breathless. "Oh my," she said.

"Indeed," he replied. He helped her stand, placing one hand lovingly against her cheek and stroking her hair with the other. "Christy, do you feel all right? Are you dizzy?"

"A...little light-headed."

"Let's get you back into the house, then. Here, you can lean on my arm."

"Thank you." She pressed into his side, and they ambled back to the house. She looked up at the stars one last time and marveled at the depth and magnitude of them. That was something she never saw in the city.

He led her to the armchair in the living room, then went to the kitchen to make some tea for her to drink. She pulled a throw rug from the settee and wrapped it around her shoulders while she waited, nestling into the soft wool. As he carried a steaming mug to her, her heart warmed at his thoughtful tenderness. He was tall, strong, with labor-calloused hands, yet lovingly tending to her every need once again. She felt her eyes prick with tears and struggled to hold them back. "Thank you, Brent. This is very thoughtful."

"Christy?"

"Yes?"

"I know you said you wanted to go back tomorrow on the train, but…"

"I don't," she interrupted. "But I thought you wanted me to."

Brent blinked several times in shock. "I… I don't want you to. So do you think…perhaps you might consider staying a while? Just to see how things go?"

"Like…a trial marriage?" Christy held the mug to her lips and blew softly on it.

"Yes, I suppose. Maybe we could…give it a go for a certain period of time, and then decide what we'd like to do? I mean…" He sighed and shook his head. "I get all tongue-tied and stammer around you, woman. I guess what I'm saying is I want you to stay." His eyes sought hers, and she could see his vulnerability.

She smiled. "I'd like to stay. Would three months suffice, do you think?"

"Three months would be good—one way or the other, we should be able to make a decision by then."

"It's settled, then," said Christy with relief. She sighed, closed her eyes and leaned back in the armchair.

Three months would give her time to figure out what it was she wanted from life. Perhaps it would even give her attorneys time to reclaim her inheritance. Three months with a guaranteed roof over her head and food in her belly—that was a fine idea. And the thought of spending it with Brent sent a flutter of nervous excitement through her stomach.

Within two weeks, Christy had found a kind of rhythm to her new life in the country. She rose early and tended to the chickens, collecting eggs for their breakfast and any baking she might do during the day. Then she'd rummage through the wild kitchen garden (growing increasingly less wild as she trimmed and weeded a little each day) for ripened vegetables.

With each passing day, she worked harder and harder to repay the kindnesses Brent had shown her. She made him a hot breakfast every morning, for which he thanked her repeatedly. One day a week she baked bread, soon followed by cakes, pies, cookies and the odd casserole. Another day each week, she did laundry. Another was set aside for ironing, still another for cleaning the house. Soon the place gleamed as best it could, given the rough nature of the building, as she scoured, scrubbed and dusted every square inch.

The rest of the week was set aside for experimenting—attempts at making soap, butter, even cheese, things she'd never done before. (If you wanted cheese in Philadelphia, there were any number of groceries and dairies to buy from.) Brent helped her by giving her the ingredients she needed and passing on an old notebook of his mother's which had some basic recipes. She was very pleased with the early results and decided to work on improving them as best she could.

On this particular morning, Christy was ironing and gazing out the window at the blowing grasses, wishing she could be outside enjoying the breeze.

Brent strode into the house. "How would you like to learn to milk a cow?" he asked, a gleam in his eye.

Christy stared in dismay at the muddy trail he'd left across the floor. "Oh dear, Brent—could you please wipe your feet on the mat before you come in?"

He stared at the rug, grimaced and quickly walked backward out the door to do just that. "Sorry, Christy. I'll have to get used to having a clean house again—or for that matter, having a doormat again." It was really just a burlap sack she had nailed to the back porch in front of the door, but it did the job. "So about the cow?"

She wiped her hands against her apron and smoothed her hair. "I guess I could try. I've never had much to do with cows, you know. Where did you get one?"

"The Harrises loaned her to me in exchange for shoeing one of their horses."

"Oh. Well, so long as you don't make me hold her still too," she said with a laugh.

Brent laughed along with her. "I won't make that mistake twice."

She followed him out the front door and to the barn, where a brown-and-white cow stood sedately, staring at them from beneath long black eyelashes and swishing her tail. "She doesn't look happy," Christy opined. "You don't think she'll kick me, do you?" She wrung her hands and hung back anxiously.

"No, I've tied her foot to the post on this side. See?"

She looked and saw a rope around the cow's back

foot, securing it loosely to the post where the beast was hitched.

Brent reached for her hand and pulled her gently toward the animal. “Come on, I’ll be right here with you. If you can take this on as one of your regular chores, I’ll probably buy her outright, so you two will get to know each other soon enough.”

Christy forced a smile and stepped forward with determination. Brent slid two squat stools close to the cow’s side. He sat on the outside one and pointed to the inside one for Christy. She lowered herself onto it and he wrapped his arms around her, reaching for the cow’s udder. She felt her cheeks flush with warmth at his touch.

“See, you reach for a teat, like so…” He grabbed one and gently pulled it toward them. “Then you hold it tight at the top, close your fingers down on it like this and pull.” As he spoke, a stream of creamy white milk spurted into the wooden bucket he’d placed beneath the creature. He repeated the movement with his other hand and soon had two long streams of milk flowing in bursts into the bucket.

“Now here, you try.” He let go of the udder and lifted Christy’s hands to it with his own. She felt her skin tingle as their fingers connected.

“All right.” She copied what Brent had been doing, but nothing happened. She squeezed, cajoled and pulled, but still no milk appeared. “What am I doing wrong?”

“Here, let me show you again.” He closed his hands around hers and she felt his fingers pulse, bringing milk down into the bucket again.

“I think I’ve got it now.” She tried again and this time the udder released a short burst of liquid. “I did it! Did you see that? I did it! I can milk a cow!" Christy beamed and she tried again. "I'm doing it!"

Brent chuckled and released his grip on her hands. She continued the movement, concentrating hard, but after a few minutes she leaned back against Brent and stopped. "I don't think I can do any more. My hands are cramping."

"I think you'll get the hang of it. You're a natural." He reached up and stroked her face, and she suddenly became very aware of how close they were, his legs on either side of her and his arms wrapped around her shoulders. She turned her head toward his with a half-smile playing on her lips.

"Christy…" She saw his eyes turn dark and he leaned toward her, his lips finding hers. The sweetness of the kiss made her shiver and she melted into his embrace, her head spinning.

Suddenly, something scratchy and damp hit her hard in the back of the head. She cried out in surprise and slipped from the stool onto the dirty barn floor with a thud. She looked up at Brent with wide eyes, wondering what on Earth had happened.

He burst out laughing, and tears soon streaked down his cheeks.

"What is so funny?" she demanded, standing to her feet and dusting her skirts.

"It was her tail…she got you in the head with her tail. I'm sorry, Christy, truly I am…" He attempted to hold in his laughter but couldn't, and soon the two of them were doubled over together.

"Excuse me, folks? Sounds to me like you're having a mite too much fun in here for common decency."

The man's voice made them both spin around to face

the open barn door. Then Brent smiled. "Clive! Good to see you." He walked over to the man and shook his hand.

Clive's eyes sparkled and he grinned at Christy. "You must be the new little lady." He went over, holding out his hand.

Christy curtsied quickly and took it. "Yes, I'm Christy Hancock… I mean, Christy Taylor. Sorry, it's still so new—I haven't introduced myself as Mrs. Taylor to anyone before now."

"Pleased to meet you. Name's Clive Harris—Kip's pa."

"Oh, of course. Kip is such a lovely boy. I've so enjoyed getting to know him."

"Well, I hope you folks don't mind, but we've come over to get acquainted with the new missus and help out around here a bit."

"We?" asked Christy, looking out the barn door—and gasping when she saw three wagons full of people in the driveway.

Clive walked out to them, and Brent and Christy followed. "This is my wife, Emily, and my children—you know Kip," Clive began. "Over there are the Hattons—Joe and Henny and their younguns. And yonder are Ed and Mary Connelly with baby Edward. We're your nearest neighbors."

"Pleased to meet all of you." Christy curtsied and nodded to the group.

The Harrises, Hattons and Connellys bundled from the wagons and milled around her asking questions, giving compliments and marveling over her red curls. Before long, the women had dragged her inside and the men had disappeared back into the barn together.

Mary Connelly was the biggest talker, with a trace of an Irish brogue not dissimilar from Christy's. "I told Ed, that poor woman is stuck in that run-down house over there. We have to go and help her clean it up. It's a travesty the way Brent let it go over the past few months. Though now that I see it, it's not so run-down after all. I love what you've done with the place, dearie!"

"Not to mention what you've done for his poor broken heart," chimed in Henny. The women all nodded and tut-tutted together.

"But if there's any way we can help, we'd love to," added Emily.

"You're all too kind," responded Christy.

"Not at all, not at all," Mary insisted. "You just tell us if we're overstepping, but I think we should start in that garden. What do you think?"

"That sounds fine," said Christy. "I've been picking away at it, but I know I have a long way to go."

They bustled Christy out the front door, where she saw the children had carried buckets, shovels, stakes, and seedling plants in clay pots from the wagon beds and laid them out beside the garden. The women and older children began weeding the rows, replanting the seedlings, and staking and trimming back the tomato and pumpkin vines and bean runners. The younger children hauled away the cut vegetable matter and occasional rocks.

After an hour, they had a garden of freshly turned, dark, moist earth and straight rows of seeds and plants. "That would have taken me forever to do on my own," said Christy, overcome with the kindness of her new neighbors.

"You're welcome," said a smiling Henny. "That's what neighbors are for 'round these parts."

"It's not how things were in Philadelphia, that's for sure."

"Welcome to the frontier," Emily said with a chuckle. She folded her hands in front of her dress, her eyes full of concern. "Brent told us you lost your parents, is that right?"

"Yes," Christy whispered. She still had trouble talking about it, the pain was too fresh.

"I'm sorry to hear that. But Brent is a wonderful man and between him and us, you're not alone in the world, don't you worry."

Christy wiped away a tear that slipped from her eyes unbidden. "Thank you."

"Now then, let's tackle the inside of the house," said Emily, wiping her hands on her gardening apron.

Christy glanced around and saw the men and boys scattered around the ranch—fixing broken fence palings, scrubbing the outside of the house. One older boy was nailing down loose floorboards on the verandah.

Inside, the women and girls got back to work—polishing, mending, sorting through the unpacked boxes in one of the unused rooms. The men came in as well once they'd finished outside, and began fixing anything broken. By the end of the day, the house looked like new and Christy found herself choking on unshed tears as she thanked the exhausted party. They clambered into their wagons and left with arms waving, calling out heartfelt goodbyes.

Chapter Seventeen

Brent tapped his pipe out on the ashtray and puffed one last breath of smoke into the still night. The wooden horse in his hands was almost finished, and he snapped closed his whittling knife and slid it into his pants pocket. Christy had retired for the evening. It had been a long October day of weeding and preparing for harvest, and his body ached from it. Livestock is so much easier, he thought as he stood and stretched.

The lowing of the cattle in the yard by the barn—he'd agreed to buy the cow, which Christy had named Bo for some reason—filled the silence, and contentment settled over his spirit. It felt good to have Christy in the house. She'd made a hearty casserole for supper, and apple cobbler with apples from the big old tree on the edge of the garden for dessert. It had been a good day.

He walked inside and locked the door. Turning down the lanterns in the living room and kitchen, he stopped to stare down the hall at Christy's closed bedroom door. Although they were officially married, they still hadn't slept in the same room, and he wondered when they might take that next step. The longing inside him seemed to grow every day, but he didn't want to push her. If she wasn't ready, he'd wait…but for how long? Likely until the three months they'd agreed to were over, which was sensible. If that was the case, it would only be a few more weeks.

It was hard to believe she'd been there for over two months already. The time had flown by, and already he couldn't imagine being here without her. The thought that she might still decide to move back to Topeka—or Philadelphia—made his heart clench with fear. The house would be so quiet and lonely without her. He couldn't go back to living like that again.

A piece of paper on the dining table caught his attention. He picked it up to read by the moonlight coming through the kitchen window. It looked like a letter from a law firm in Philadelphia, addressed to Christy—something about her inheritance from a Mr. Hancock (her father?) being challenged. It stated that the case was expected to be resolved within the next month. It was dated a few weeks earlier.

Brent felt guilt wash over him. He shouldn't have read it—and if he'd known it was a private letter to Christy, he wouldn't have. But now that he'd seen it, he couldn't help feeling curious. Was she due an inheritance from her parents? She hadn't mentioned one. If that were the case, perhaps she was only staying with him until it came through and she'd be able to take care of herself.

He'd gotten the sense that Christy was warming to him and the idea of living with him at the ranch. At first, he'd been concerned she'd never be able to adjust to country life, but she'd adapted quickly and even seemed to be enjoying it. She had certainly made fast friendships with the other farmers' wives, especially Emily Harris. But what if she was just biding her time until her inheritance came through and she was able to afford a ticket elsewhere? She'd mentioned when she first arrived that she couldn't manage a train ticket back to Pennsylvania. Maybe that's all she was waiting for.

Brent walked to one of the otherwise empty bedrooms, where he'd finally set up a cot, and sat on it to remove his boots. He set his hat on a nearby box and lay back on top of the blankets, still dressed. God, I don't want her to leave, he prayed. I don't want to live without her. I can't go back to being all alone out here. She doesn't know how I feel about her. Help me to show her.

Christy woke with a start. A noise had wakened her. She listened for it in case it came again.

There it was—a knock at her door. "Christy!" Brent called quietly through it.

"Yes."

"Did you still wish to go to church with me this morning?"

"Oh, that's right. Yes, I do."

"Well, we'll need to leave in about a half-hour."

"Thank you." Christy pushed back the covers and climbed from the still-warm bed. The chill of the dark morning air made her want to snuggle back in, but she forced herself to get up, light a lantern and wash and dress quickly. When she opened the curtains, she could see the sun rising over the prairie behind the barn, bringing the birds out to carol and twitter in the yard. She joined Brent in the kitchen for a quick breakfast of hot coffee and bread. While she cleaned up, he hurried outside to hitch Patty to the wagon.

Christy was excited to see the church. They hadn't attended since she'd been there, since Brent had wanted her to settle in before introducing her around Newton. She was anxious to meet more people and reacquaint herself with the whirl of society. But Brent seemed quieter than usual as they rode, so she took the time to enjoy the beautiful scenery. And the proximity—she rarely got the chance to sit so close to Brent. His tall frame dwarfed hers, and she felt safe beside him.

The church building was a small white chapel on a hill outside the town. As they drew close, she could see wagons and buggies winding up the long driveway and parking on the hillside around the building. Their wagon soon joined the throng.

They pulled to a halt beside the chapel and Brent climbed down, offering her his arm. She'd worn her best green muslin gown with the thin black cross-hatch pattern, and a matching green-and-black hat. Her red hair was piled on top of her head and spilled out in ringlets. Brent smiled up at her as she descended, a gleam of approval in his blue eyes. She waited patiently while Brent tended to his horse, then they walked into the church together.

"Christy, Brent, hello!" called Emily, hurrying toward them with her blonde curls bouncing. "So glad you two made it. Come and sit with Clive and me." She led the way and they found Clive, Kip and the other children in a pew near the front of the church.

The service was enjoyable and Christy found herself reveling in being around people again, even those she didn't know. She'd never been as isolated from society as she was living on the ranch, and was glad there were other women here she could relate to. Emily introduced her around, and she was happy to see Henny and Mary there as well.

This place was becoming more of a home to her than Philadelphia could be with her parents gone. She knew her feelings for Brent had grown in the time she'd spent there and that she didn't want to leave him. But did he feel the same way? She looked at him, seated beside her, his rugged good looks sending a thrill through her. He turned to smile at her, and she felt her cheeks flush.

After the service closed, people stood up to mill around and fellowship. "Clive and Emily asked if we'd like to have lunch at their ranch," Brent told her. "What do you think?"

"That sounds lovely. Only I didn't bring anything..."

"Oh, that's all right—Emily said we didn't need to."

"How kind."

"Shall I tell them yes?"

"Yes, please do."

Brent walked over to speak with Clive while Christy surveyed the room. It was only a small group, but they all seemed to know each other well. While she waited, several more women came by to introduce themselves and make her feel welcome.

He soon returned and helped Christy into the wagon. "What did you think of it?" he asked once they were on their way.

"I enjoyed it. The message was lively and the people are very friendly. I'm looking forward to getting to know them all."

"I'm glad to hear that. I'd hoped we might be able to attend every week, weather permitting."

"That sounds fine." She looped her hand through

Brent's arm and leaned against his shoulder. He grinned at her and clicked his tongue at Patty.

Christy didn't know what her future might hold, but in that moment she was filled with deep contentment. And Brent's plan for attending church—he'd said "we," as if planning on having her around. That was a good sign, wasn't it? She closed her eyes and listened to Patty's hoofbeats and the turning of the wagon wheels along the dusty track.

Chapter Eighteen

"I thought we might go into town today."

"Oh?" Christy took a bite of her oatmeal and chewed thoughtfully. She'd only been into Newton once if one didn't count church—and that was the day she'd arrived. That had all been such a blur, she didn't have much chance to see the sights. She'd like to see it now that she'd settled in. And it was a beautiful Saturday morning.

"There's a dance at the meeting hall this afternoon. I thought you might like to go." Brent bit into a thick slice of fresh bread and chewed thoughtfully as he watched her face for a reaction.

Her eyes grew wide and she clapped her hands together in glee. "A dance! Yes, please. I'd love to go to a dance. Will Emily, Henny and Mary be there?"

"I'd imagine so. We don't have too many dances around here. Also, I've got a few errands to run in town, and you could take a look around the mercantile to see if there's anything you need. What do you say?"

Christy squealed in response and jumped up to lean across the table and kiss Brent on the forehead. He laughed and pulled her down for a kiss on the mouth, upsetting her oatmeal in the process.

"Oh dear, what a mess," said Christy, pulling away to hurry into the kitchen for a damp cloth. She felt the heat rising to her face. A dance—she hadn't attended a dance since the New Year's Ball in Philadelphia. And she knew just which dress she could wear. She couldn't wait.

As she came back with the cloth, a thought struck her. "Do we have to bring anything?" She knew that married women usually brought food to community events.

"I suppose so. Not really sure, myself."

"Well, I baked that raisin cake last night, so that should do well enough. Oh, how exciting! I'd better go and get ready—I assume we'll be leaving soon?"

"Soon as we can," Brent agreed. He left to prepare the horse and wagon.

Christy quickly cleaned up the breakfast things and packed up the cake, some lunch and other items they might need for the day. Then she went into the bedroom and changed into a forest-green velvet dress with lace around the collars and cuffs, and a matching hat and parasol. She smoothed her hair back into a neat chignon and hurried outside to meet Brent, ready to enjoy her day on the town.

Newton was a small, dusty town, and on this Saturday a bustling one. Christy surveyed the main street—almost the only street—as they went trotting down it in their open wagon. There were a few stores on either side with swinging signs advertising their wares, a smithy, the sheriff's office, a school, and a long saloon with a brightly painted sign right in the middle. Not bad for a town that hadn't even existed six months before.

As they passed the saloon, Christy was horrified to see men with scantily-clad women leaning out of open windows, their drunken laughter and shouts echoing throughout the town. "Is it always like this?" she asked.

"What? Do you mean the saloon? Well, I suppose."

Christy sniffed and tightened her mouth.

"Hello, Brent! Hi there, honey!" a brunette called from one of the windows, her long braid hanging over one exposed shoulder.

"Oh, uh…hello, Prissy." Brent ducked his head in embarrassment.

"You know her?" asked Christy.

"Not really, no. I went in there a couple of times when I first got here, just to be around people, and she was serving drinks. But I haven't been in since you arrived. Um…"

Christy wasn't sure what to think. Brent did come to town on his own about once a week. Maybe he was going to the saloon to see Prissy—or do more than just see her. She shook her head in disbelief. After all they'd been through together, with how they were drawing closer to each other every day, surely he wouldn't do that. But it reminded her once again that there was much she didn't know about her new husband.

Smith's Mercantile was a cluttered mess—products of various types scattered in bunches and piles in a seemingly random fashion throughout the floor space. Christy and Brent entered through the front door and a bell rang softly overhead to announce their arrival.

"Good morning, Mr. Taylor," said an older woman

who stood behind a long counter against the left wall of the store.

"Mrs. Cuthbert, how are you today?"

"Well, thank you. And you?"

"I'm fine. This is my wife, Christy." Brent placed his hand in the small of Christy's back and smiled down at her.

"How lovely to meet you." Mrs. Cuthbert came out from behind the counter with her hand outstretched, took Christy's hand in her own and shook it. "We're all so glad Mr. Taylor's found a wife. It was so very sad the way he lost Annabelle—I assume you know about Annabelle?"

"Yes, of course. Thank you—it's nice to meet you as well."

"Christy said she'd like to look around a bit. I'm going in back to see Steve—I need to order some horse feed and a few other things." Brent turned and left.

Mrs. Cuthbert slipped behind the counter. "Well, I imagine you don't need clothes, if that lovely frock you're wearing is any indication. Where did you get that?"

Christy smiled. "Wanamaker's Grand Depot. I'm originally from Philadelphia."

"Land sakes, you've made a journey, haven't you? I got to visit Philly a couple of times—Steve and I are from Ocean City, New Jersey, by way of St. Louis."

"Really? I spent a lovely summer week in Ocean City when I was twelve!" That got them talking in earnest about places they both knew back East. Soon Mrs. Cuthbert brought out tea and homemade ginger snaps, Christy sat on a stool on the customer side of the counter and they gabbed like old friends, interrupted only when

Mrs. Cuthbert served a couple of Cherokee women, who traded some homemade blankets for other items. After they left, Christy asked, "Do you get a lot of Indian custom here?"

"Oh, some. Steve doesn't like it—he always calls them 'savages'—but they seem like nice enough folks to me. My only rule is I won't sell them whiskey—I've heard their men can't handle it too well. But otherwise, I've never had a problem with them. And people sure do like these blankets they weave—we make a lot of money from them."

By the time Brent returned, Christy had purchased one of the blankets, done in varying shades of blue, along with a hairbrush, some cakes of soap (her experiments on that score were still uneven), a washtub, a string of garlic bulbs and—for Brent—a bolo tie with a big chunk of turquoise for a clasp. She hurried over to her husband and put it around his neck. "There. How do you like it?"

Brent was pleasantly surprised. "For me? Well, thank you—you didn't have to get me anything."

"I wanted to."

Mrs. Cuthbert grinned. "You've got yourself a lovely wife there, Mr. Taylor. I look forward to seeing you again, Christy!"

"And you too," Christy replied. She didn't say that while she definitely wanted to, it would be up to Brent whether she could.

The space around the meeting hall was filled with empty wagons and picketed horses, the latter grazing and resting beneath a large oak. Christy and Brent made their way inside, stopping to greet those they knew along the way. Brent seemed to appreciate her dress. It floated around her legs, and her corset and petticoats gave her curves a boost that drew eyes her way as they walked.

The band—an upright piano and two fiddles—began to play as Christy set her cake on a long table already filled with delicious food. "Shall we dance?" asked Brent, bowing with a twinkle in his eye.

"I'd love to."

He drew her out to the dance floor and held her close as they waltzed with several other couples over the worn floorboards. Christy leaned into his embrace, and the room around them swirled and then disappeared as she gazed into his blue eyes.

After that song ended, a man tapped Brent on the shoulder and cut in. She didn't recognize him, but he led her in an energetic two-step that had her laughing and out of breath by the end. Then Clive Harris cut in, and she found herself being whirled around the dance floor again.

When she had the chance, she looked around the room for Brent and found him standing by the food table, eating from a piled-high plate. She wished he were here on the dance floor with his arms wrapped around her again. It was fun dancing with the other men, but what she really wanted was to dance with Brent. The feel of his embrace sent a thrill through her every time.

She earnestly hoped that he wasn't hiding anything from her, like spending time at the saloon with that Prissy woman. She wanted to trust him, but she wasn't sure she knew him well enough yet. Just when she felt as though she did, something else would come up to make her second-guess everything.

Finally, the song was over and Christy bid Clive farewell, found a chair against the wall and flopped into it. Dancing was a lot of fun, but it had been too long since she'd done it and it was taking a lot out of her. She pulled out a handkerchief and wiped the beading sweat from her brow.

Mary and Emily hurried over to sit beside her. "Christy, how are you? How's the house working out for you?"

"And the garden?"

"And Brent?" Henny, trailing the group, chimed in. They hammered her with questions, all eager to find out how things were going at the ranch.

Christy laughed. "Things are going very well. Brent is kind and thoughtful. The house is amazing, and the garden is growing like crazy. Thank you all so much for everything you did. It helped us immensely."

"Never mind that. How are things between you and Brent?" asked Henny, leaning forward with a grin.

"Henny!" exclaimed Emily, slapping her wrist.

"What? We all want to know. The lone stallion has finally been tamed! Tell us everything."

"The…lone stallion?" asked Christy, with arched eyebrows.

"Brent has something of a reputation," Mary explained. "Nothing bad, mind you. He's just so handsome, and he was about the only young man in town who came here without a family. And you know how gossipers—" She glanced briefly at Henny. "—go on. A few women tried to entice him, but he was never interested in that sort of thing. So of course everyone's curious about you—the woman who finally won him over."

"Really?" Christy frowned. The description did sound like Brent, and she supposed that with no other eligible men in the area he might easily end up a sought-after beau. Still, the whole incident with Prissy had her concerned. "Things between us are mostly good. I mean, we're still getting to know each other, but I really like him."

"I should hope so—you're married to him," chuckled Mary.

"Yes, but we were married the first day we met, so it's an unusual situation."

"Why only mostly good?" asked Henny.

Should she tell them? Well, she needed to talk to somebody about it… "Well, when we drove through town earlier, one of the saloon girls called out to him as though she knew him."

"Ah yes, those saloon girls. They know just about every man in town and out of it. He's likely had a drink or a meal there—there aren't many men around these parts who haven't."

"Is that true?" asked Christy.

"Yes, unfortunately." Emily grimaced. "Clive went once, and I told him he'd better not do it again."

"But just because Brent's been to the saloon doesn't mean anything," Mary assured Christy. "He may have only gone there for a drink, or just to be around people."

"That's what he said when I asked him."

"Well, there you go, lass. That's probably it."

"I hope so." But Christy wished she could be sure.

When the dance was over and everyone had eaten their fill, they all bundled into their wagons and buggies and headed home. The sun was setting across the plains, its golden light bathing the settlers in a fiery blaze of pinks, oranges and yellows.

"Do you think you could hold Patty's reins while I fix the traces?" asked Brent, one eyebrow raised.

"I'll try," answered Christy.

He led the horse to her and handed her the reins, then began attaching the horse to the wagon. The bay lifted one of his back hooves and held it above the ground, as though he didn't want to put it down.

"What's this?" Brent took the leg and looked closely at the hoof. "It looks like he has a thorn in the frog. I'll have to get it out—hold tight."

Christy gripped the reins tightly and gritted her teeth. Brent pulled the thorn out with a grunt, and the beast's head flung upwards, striking Christy under the chin and making her see stars. But while she cried out, she didn't let go of the reins. "Silly old Patty, hold steady there," she admonished the horse, stroking the length of his face.

Brent looked at her in surprise and pride. "Thanks, Christy. Are you all right? That must have smarted."

"I'm fine, I think." She blinked a few times to clear her head.

He smiled at her. "You're becoming a real rancher's wife, you know that?"

"I guess I am." Top that, Prissy, she thought.

Chapter Nineteen

Monday dawned bright and sunny, with only a few fluffy clouds on the horizon. Christy sighed in contentment as she collected the eggs from the henhouse. The dance on Saturday had been the highlight of her week, and church on Sunday was a blessing as well. She was already looking forward to the church scavenger hunt that they'd announced for the following month. But to attend, she'd have to stay past the three-month trial period. Was that what she wanted?

Part of her longed to return home, but only because she missed her parents and the life they'd had there. Going back to Philadelphia wouldn't bring them back. She also knew that she had to accept what her mother had told her, that part of life was embracing change, wanted or not. There was no way but forward.

She wandered inside and placed the eggs in a bowl on the kitchen table. As she began preparing breakfast, Brent strode in from the barn where he'd just finished his morning chores. "What do you think about a picnic after church?"

"A picnic? Where?"

"We could ride out to Red Rock Canyon. It's not far from here and I think you'd like it."

"But I don't know how to ride."

"And you could learn. I've got an old mare, Sally, and she won't go faster than a trot. You'll be fine—and I'll be with you the whole time. What do you say?"

She gave it some thought. "That sounds lovely. Shall I pack some sandwiches?"

"Good idea. I'll go get the horses ready."

Sally swayed from side to side, walking slowly, her dappled gray coat dull beneath the morning sun. Christy scanned the horizon, delighting in the tall, waving prairie grasses and the peaked shadows of a distant mountain range.

"How are you doing?" asked Brent, slowing Patty to ride beside Christy on Sally.

"Very well, I think. You were right, Sally is gentle."

"Yes, she's an old sweetie. She won't give you any trouble."

"Did you know that we have only less than two weeks before the end of our trial marriage?" asked Christy, squinting through the sunshine at Brent's tanned face.

He shot her a sidelong glance. "That soon, huh?"

"I know, it's hard to believe. It's gone by quickly, don't you think?"

"Sure has."

Christy sighed and rolled her eyes. Sometimes she had to work so hard to extract anything from him. He'd never told her how he felt about her, or whether he wanted her to stay. She hoped he'd say something before the time was up—she really wanted to make plans. If he decided he didn't want to stay married, she'd have to figure out what she would do and where she could go. But she hoped he did want her to stay, because of how she'd grown to care about him.

Before long, Brent pulled Patty to a stop, stood in his stirrups and pointed ahead. "There it is. That's the canyon up ahead."

Christy leaned forward over Sally's neck. She could see the grasses give way and a massive crack in the earth opened up before them. Its brick-red sides jutted downward, sheer as the walls of an ancient fortress.

"Let's leave the horses here and walk the rest of the way," suggested Brent.

They dismounted and pegged the horses under a redbud tree where they could graze. Taking the picnic basket under one arm and offering the other to Christy, Brent led the way down to the canyon's edge.

It wasn't a large canyon, now that she could see it more closely. But it was still spectacular, the cliff faces dropping to a rocky floor below. "It's beautiful," said Christy as she laid out the blanket for them to sit on. She pulled sandwiches, fruit slices and cookies from the basket.

Brent sat close beside her and lifted his hand to trace the line of her cheek. "You look beautiful. I don't tell you that often enough."

Christy smiled at him and rested her cheek in his hand for a moment, her eyes closing with the pleasure of his touch. "You can tell me that anytime you feel the need."

"I will."

"Let's eat, shall we?"

"It looks delicious and I'm famished."

Christy handed Brent a sandwich and they ate quietly,

looking out over the gaping chasm in the earth. A hawk soared above the canyon, its keen eyes searching for prey while it climbed on an updraft.

"It's so beautiful out here," said Christy.

"Yes, it is. It's so different from Kentucky, but I love it just the same."

"I spent my entire life in cities, so everything here is new to me. But I'm growing to like it too."

Brent was silent for a moment. "Is there anywhere you've always wanted to go?"

"Not really. I never thought much about traveling until Mam and Daddy decided to move to California. Now, I feel as though I should go there sometime, just to finish what they started."

Brent's eyes clouded over and he dropped his eyes to the picnic blanket beneath them.

"I don't mean move there," she added hastily, "just visit sometime. I'm not even sure why—maybe to say goodbye to them in my own way."

Brent looked up at her hopefully. "That makes sense."

Christy's heart ached to tell him she wanted him to go with her, but she couldn't get the words out. Instead, she took another bite of her sandwich and stared up into the sky. "Wouldn't it be amazing to be able to fly like that hawk?"

"Hmmm...you like to be free, huh?" Brent stood up, wandered over to Patty and stroked the horse's neck while he finished his sandwich.

Christy shook her head in dismay. What had she said to upset him? Sometimes she wondered just what was going on inside his head.

Chapter Twenty

Hoofbeats thundered up the driveway and into the barn where Christy was milking Bo. It was the last day of the trial marriage, and she found herself humming nervously as she worked. She stood and wiped her hands clean on her apron as she walked to the barn door, to find Clive Harris leaping from the back of a prancing chestnut stallion. "Mornin', Christy. How are you on this fine day?"

"I'm well, thank you, Clive," she lied. "And you?"

"Just fine and dandy. I have somethin' for you. I went to town yesterday and collected our mail, and the clerk had a telegram for you." He reached into his shirt pocket, fished out a folded piece of paper and handed it to her.

"Thank you, Clive. Let me see..." Christy unfolded the paper.

Christy Hancock. Inheritance resolved in your favor. Money wired to Topeka National Bank as requested. Please write with further instructions. More details on way via mail. Smythe, Esq.

Christy sighed in relief and held the telegram to her

chest. She closed her eyes and offered up a prayer of thanksgiving.

"Good news, I hope?" said Clive, shuffling his feet in the dust.

"Very good news. Thank you for delivering this."

"You're welcome. I can't stay—harvest time, you know. Tell Brent howdy for me." He climbed back onto the chestnut and, with a tip of his hat, cantered back down the drive toward his own ranch.

Christy felt as though a great weight had been lifted from her shoulders. She raised her arms skyward and twirled in a circle with her eyes closed and her face lifted to the heavens. She had hoped this day would come, and now it finally had.

Even though she'd never really wanted for anything since her parents died and God had provided all she needed, having the legal issues around her inheritance resolved gave her some measure of closure over her parents' death. She didn't really understand why, but having her inheritance taken from her would have made her feel as though she was even further disconnected from them. Having the house in Philadelphia and the small nest egg was a way for her to hold onto them for a while longer.

She ran into the house in search of Brent to tell him the good news. She found him in the kitchen, pouring himself a cup of steaming, black coffee. "Brent, good news! I…" She stopped short. All of a sudden, she realized that she had never told Brent about her legal issues and wasn't sure how to broach the subject.

"What is it, Christy? Did I hear a horse outside?"

"Yes, it was Clive. He brought me a telegram from town."

"Oh? What was the telegram about?"

"I'm sorry I never told you this before now, but there were some legal issues with my parents' estate. Relatives of mine in Ireland contested the will—they claimed the inheritance should be theirs and that I should come to live under their guardianship. I have no idea why they thought that—perhaps they were trying to protect me… anyway, the telegram is from Daddy's lawyer, saying the issue's been resolved in my favor. I've inherited my parents' estate in its entirety. Isn't it wonderful? It's as though I've been traveling around with this cloud over my head and now the sun is shining! I feel free for the first time since they died!"

Brent's lips tightened and his eyes clouded over. "That's…good news, Christy. I'm happy for you."

Christy was confused. Why didn't he look happy? Perhaps he didn't understand what she was saying. "It's not a large amount of money, but there's the house in Philadelphia and enough money for me to live off for a while. I'm just so relieved. It's the last thing I have of theirs—I know it probably doesn't make sense, but it feels as if I can hold onto a piece of them now."

Brent went to her, laid a hand on her shoulder and looked deep into her eyes. "I'm glad, Christy. It's what you deserve." Then he strode from the house, shoved his Stetson on his head and disappeared toward the horse yard.

Within a few minutes, Christy could hear Patty's hooves on the driveway as he galloped off. Where is he off to? Why is he acting so strangely? What on Earth is going on with him today? She sighed and stamped her foot in frustration. Sometimes she didn't understand Brent at all.

* * *

Brent leaned over Patty's neck and urged him forward. The horse responded, laying his ears back and galloping across the field. He was headed toward town, but as he reached the main road, he pulled Patty to a halt. He needed time to think, and the best place he'd found for that was Red Rock Canyon. He wheeled the horse around and set off that way instead.

Before long, he reached the chasm, slipped from Patty's back and let the reins drop to the ground. Patty would stay close, grazing on the autumn prairie grasses. He sat at the edge of one of the cliff faces and stared out over the landscape. The beauty of the rugged scene always calmed his spirit and helped him think more clearly.

He'd been concerned this day would come. Ever since he found that letter about Christy's inheritance, he knew that one day she might not need him any longer. And today it was all over her face. She was relieved. She was free. She didn't need him to take care of her now. She would go home now that she could afford to. He was certain of it.

He lay back and stared up into the sky. He didn't want her to leave. His life was so much better with her in it. He had to tell her how he felt. He couldn't let her go without at least pleading his case. They were good together. They were happy. He couldn't believe that she didn't feel it as well. And when they kissed, it was as though a bolt of lightning jolted him, sending pleasure crashing through him every time.

No, he couldn't let her go. Not without a fight.

He jumped to his feet and hurried back to Patty.

With a leap, he landed on the horse's back and wheeled him around to head back to the ranch. He had to see Christy before she made up her mind to leave and he lost her for good.

Chapter Twenty-One

Christy lifted the heavy saddle onto Sally's back and with an effort cinched the girth strap tight. She jerked on the saddle to make sure it held, and it did. "Good. Now what next?"

A bridle hung on the wall of the barn, and she lifted it from the nail holding it in place and carried it back to where Sally stood waiting. She slipped it over Sally's ears and pushed the bit gently between her teeth. But when she attempted to climb onto Sally's back, the old gray mare walked forward, almost sending Christy tumbling to the ground. She grabbed a handful of mane and sat quickly in the saddle, adjusting herself into the sidesaddle position and smoothing her skirts over her legs.

With a click of her tongue, she steered Sally out, and they set off at a walk across the field. She didn't know where she was going, only that she needed time to think. Brent had left hours ago and not returned. Perhaps he'd gone to the saloon in town to whisper sweet nothings in Prissy's ear. The thought filled her with anger, and she shook her head. No, he wouldn't do that. She knew him. She had to trust him. He had told her he didn't go to the saloon anymore, and as far as she knew he'd never done anything to break her trust, never lied to her in the three months they'd spent together. She had to hold onto that.

What she really needed, now that she had options, was to consider them and decide what she wanted to do with her life. She really could go anywhere or do anything she wanted. So...what did she want?

She passed the spot near the creek where she'd been ambushed by the prairie dog when she first arrived, and carefully steered Sally around the burrows pockmarking the field. It would be disastrous for Sally to step into one of those holes—she could break her leg and might injure Christy in the process. Past that, the flat prairie opened out before her, the yellowing lengths of grass swaying in the gentle breeze.

Christy closed her eyes and soaked up the silence and sunshine. This was beautiful country, and she'd grown to love the vast wilderness in the short time she'd lived on the ranch. It was hard to imagine returning to the city now. The idea of giving up the cozy house, the chicken coop, Bo and Sally, made her heart ache. But it was thinking about leaving Brent that brought tears to her eyes.

She knew she had to consider her friends back home. Candice had written her a letter a week, begging her to come back to Philadelphia. And with money, she could study to become a teacher. No doubt she could find a nice place to board, or just live in Mama and Daddy's old house, and return to the life she'd left behind with minimal fuss.

But she knew in that moment, deep in her heart, that she didn't want to leave Newton, or the ranch, or most of all Brent. This was her home now. She loved it here, and she loved him.

I love him. The realization hit her like a slap of truth in the face. When had it happened? Was it that first day, when he fixed her trunk and drew her a warm bath? Was it on their picnic, or at the dance? Was it when he patiently taught her to milk Bo? Or was it just a gradual descent, where each and every moment of the past three months had drawn her deeper and deeper into love?

She turned Sally around and headed back toward the ranch. She could see it in the distance, its low-peaked roof sheltering the sprawling building. The wide verandah shaded the windows and the prosperous garden lined the front with green leaves and vibrant flowers. Home. It was her home, and her heart warmed at the sight of it.

It was time she told Brent how she felt. He had to know that she loved him and wanted to stay.

Brent pulled Patty to a halt beside the barn and threw the reins around a fence post. He jumped to the ground and ran into the house, careful to wipe his feet on the doormat. "Christy!"

No response. At this time of day she was usually in the kitchen fixing lunch, but she was nowhere to be seen. He hurried through the house, calling her name in every room. She was gone. Where could she be? Surely she couldn't have left already, without saying goodbye? He felt his throat tighten as he ran outside. Oh, there she was—riding Sally into the barn. He sighed in relief and hurried after her.

She turned to greet him with a smile and he ran straight to her, pulling her from the horse's back and into his arms in a tender embrace. "Christy, there you are. I was worried. I didn't know where you were."

She looked at him in confusion. "I just took Sally out for a ride. And I didn't know where you were."

He laughed and smoothed the hair from her forehead, gazing into her green eyes with wonder. "You've never done that before. I guess this means you're comfortable riding on your own now?"

"I suppose. Is that all right?"

"It's wonderful."

"Are you…upset with me about something, Brent? When you left earlier, you seemed angry."

"No, it's just that…well, now you have your inheritance, so I imagine you'll want to go home to be with your friends and get back to your old life…" He watched her face carefully, hoping for a sign that he was wrong.

She furrowed her brow. "Oh, Brent Taylor, you silly man. This is my home."

He felt his cheeks flush with warmth, his lungs expand, as though he was finally coming up from under a deep heavy sea. "You're not going back to Philadelphia? Or Topeka?"

"Not unless you're coming with me. Well… I may need to go to Topeka to collect my inheritance. Unless I can have them transfer it here—is there a bank in Newton?"

"Nearest one's up in Deer City," he replied numbly. "One stop up the rail line."

"Well, that would make it easy. But otherwise… well, today is officially the last day of our probationary marriage—and I know my choice. What do you want?"

"I want you to stay here. With me."

"You do?"

"Of course I do. I love you, Christy Taylor. You're my wife and I want you with me."

Christy pressed her forehead against his and smiled. "Then I'm yours. I love you too, Brent Taylor."

Brent laughed and pulled back to look at her, his eyes dark with emotion. "You have made me the happiest man alive." Then he drew her close again, one hand on the small of her back, the other cupping her face in his palm. Their lips pressed together for a passionate kiss, filled with a love and tenderness that sent his head spinning.

He loved her. And she loved him.

"So what now?" Christy asked when they broke the kiss.

"Now I spend the rest of my life showing you how much I love you. I'll take care of you and I'll make sure you have all the happiness you deserve. Forever."

* * * * *

Historical Note & Author's Remarks

When I started writing this book, the Mail Order Bride genre was new to me. It started out as a short story that began in Boston and ended in Oklahoma. I've always loved historical novels and stories, and studied history extensively in college. So, writing in the historical romance genre naturally appealed to me. Stories of strong women throughout history especially grab my attention, and I liked the idea of following a series of women who find themselves alone in the world, and with few options. They each choose marriage to a stranger, to give them a new chance at life.

Real-life stories of the Mail Order Brides in the old west are fascinating. There were so many different, and varied, reasons why women chose that life, especially with the lack of eligible men in the east after The War Between The States. And of course, the men of the west found themselves surrounded by other men, women of ill repute, or married women—single women generally didn't travel west. So, a Mail Order Bride became the only chance of finding a wife for so many men at that time in history.

I first published this story as a short read. Over time, I received feedback and reviews from my readers asking for more, and so the story has been extended and re-written as a novel. I hope that you enjoy the newly extended version. It's the first in the *Orphan Brides Go West* series of four books. Each book in the series is a stand-alone novel, and each one is set in a different location in the old west. What they have in common is that the women in each book are left alone, without family to help them, and with the potential for further disaster to befall them unless they embrace significant change. They each become *Mail Order Brides*, out of desperation and with some hope for a better future.

I hope you enjoy them all!

With love,
Vivi xx

About the Author

Vivi Holt was born in Australia. She grew up in the country, where she spent her youth riding horses at Pony Club, and adventuring through the fields and rivers around the farm. Her father was a builder, turned saddler, and her mother a nurse, who stayed home to raise their four children.

After graduating from a degree in International Relations, Vivi moved to Atlanta, Georgia to work for a year. It was there that she met her husband, and they were married three years later. She spent seven years living in Atlanta and travelled to various parts of the United States during that time, falling in love with the beauty of that immense country and the American people.

Vivi also studied for a Bachelor of Information Technology, and worked in the field ever since until becoming a full-time writer in 2016. She now lives in Brisbane, Australia with her husband and three small children. Married to a Baptist pastor, she is very active in her local church.

Follow Vivi Holt
www.viviholt.com
vivi@viviholt.com

RAMONA

Chapter One

October 28, 1886
Ramona

Ramona Selmer leaned back against a sturdy pile on Pier A, and gazed out over the New York harbor. The water lapped soothingly against the shore below, sending a cool breeze up through the gaps between the boards of the pier. An enormous statue across the harbor gleamed brilliantly across the water, and Ramona squinted against the glare of the sunlight reflecting off its surface. The copper-tinted lady liberty stood tall and proud, waving a flame above her graceful head, which was crowned in long spikes while one arm cradled a book. The statue had opened officially today, dedicated to the people of New York City, a gift from the state of France. Although Ramona had been watching the progress on the construction of the statue every chance she got in the year since it had arrived by boat from France, her excitement had swelled during the past few days as the unveiling approached. The entire landscape of the New York harbor had changed because of this one piece of art, and people lingered along the shoreline gazing at it and pointing with soft smiles. Ramona loved its name—the Statue of Liberty. It was a marvelous day. A day that was a long time coming, and Ramona had relished every single celebratory moment of it.

Pushing herself to her feet, she sighed dreamily and, taking one last glance at the statue perched on the tiny Liberty Island, began to make her way back down Broadway Street. She had to get moving if she was to get to her audition on time and then home to the West Village for dinner. She also wanted to do a quick walk down the long line of theaters on Broadway, as she always did when she was in the city. Broadway was her dream. She'd taken dance, voice, and drama lessons every chance she got from when she was four years old. And ever since she could remember she'd auditioned for every show on and off Broadway that she could find.

Ramona's mother had worked hard over the years, scraping together the money for formal lessons whenever possible. The rest of the time Ramona practiced at the park with friends, or in their tiny apartment. At the age of nineteen she was starting to despair whether she would ever realize her ambitions, but her father had encouraged her not to give up hope. He'd called her his little Broadway star. And so she kept the dream alive, fanning the flame whenever possible by tramping down Broadway Street and staring at the colorful posters, and through the doorways imagining what lay within. Picturing herself the star of a hit show, her fans lined up at the door waiting to catch a glimpse of a graceful pirouette or plié.

Ramona skipped past the theaters, a small satchel bouncing on one shoulder. She stopped at an intersection and sighed deeply, taking one last look down the street at the sparkling foyers and colorful posters, and turned down a side alley. She pushed her way through a thick, red timber door and into a darkened room. It took a few moments for her eyes to adjust to the dimness, but once they did she could see the outline of the small, musty theater. Black shadows of the backs of empty chairs lined the space, row upon row, and in the front sat three figures who were perched forward watching a young girl tap dance across the stage followed closely by a yellow spotlight. As Ramona made her way to the front of the room, the song ended and the girl's dance was over. She tick-tacked off the stage, and the three men seated in the front row shuffled papers and murmured together quietly. One of the men lifted his head and spun it back and forth, shouting "Ramona Selmer?"

Ramona ran quickly to stand in front of the stage.

"Yes, sir. I'm here."

"Great. When you're ready, Ramona."

He smiled at her, then returned to writing in his notebook. His round spectacles were perched on the end of a long, pointy nose, and his waistcoat was partially unbuttoned. Ramona walked to the side of the stage, and up the stairs, her heart pounding loudly in her chest. Sitting down, she quickly removed her shoes. Reaching into her shoulder satchel she pulled out a pair of pink, scuffed ballet flats. She smoothed her long skirts, and removed her sandals, then pulled the slippers on over the pale pink stockings that covered her legs and feet. Ramona stood quickly and delivered the sheet music she had been carrying in her satchel to the pianist. Laying her satchel down on the side of the stage, she walked confidently to center stage with a smile on her face.

Ramona brushed her hair behind her shoulder. She wanted the director to see her face. Maybe he'd remember her then. As she waited for the music to begin, she lifted her arms in a graceful pose and tilted her head to stare at the seats in the back of the room. For a single moment, she felt like a glamorous Broadway star, dancing in a theater filled to capacity with elegant folks, out for a night on the town, their shining dresses, sparkling jewels and bright faces lighting up the night. All of them had bought tickets to be here. All of them were here to see her, Ramona. They had come to hear her sing, to watch her dance, to cry with her over some tragedy and to celebrate with her when she found love.

Glamour was what Ramona craved. There was little of it to be found in her life off stage, in the one bedroom West Village apartment she shared with her mother, Maria. But on stage things were different. When she was on the stage, she could be anything or anyone she wanted to be. The music began, and Ramona's lithe frame floated across the stage, leaping and spinning as she performed the routine she'd rehearsed a hundred times. Her movements slowed as she opened her mouth to sing a lilting song, full of longing and sorrow.

She danced and sang as though everything she had done for the past fifteen years was in preparation for this moment. Her chance to audition for this show. Under her feet the boards shook and creaked but her voice held steady. Her soaring soprano filled the room, the sweet notes hitting the back of the auditorium as Ramona closed her eyes and let her voice shine. She raised her arms and threw her head back dramatically for the final note, letting it hang in the air about her.

The casting directors turned to each other and whispered, casting furtive glances at the girl waiting so earnestly on stage. Finally the man with the spectacles leaned forward and gave his appraisal. "You have a beautiful voice Ramona. And it's almost there."

Ramona cupped one hand above her eyes, to shield them from the glare of the spotlight.

"Yes?" Her large brown eyes opened wide. "I know I can manage the part, if you just give me a shot. I'll work so hard, really I will."

"Maybe next year, dear. You can come back then and try again," he said, while his colleagues stared at the notebooks on their laps and studiously avoided Ramona's gaze.

Ramona nodded and left the stage, thanking the directors for their time.

Next year.

Ramona took a deep breath and held her head high. Those words were something to cling to, at least. She pushed her way through the heavy door and stumbled out into the fresh fall evening. Next year. That would give her a year to practice, perfect and hone her craft. Of course I'll be twenty by then, and practically an old maid in Broadway terms! She trudged along the pavement as she headed through downtown New York, her long dark curls and dancer's silhouette illuminated by the street lamps that were coming on all over town as the dusk of evening crept in from the bay. She shivered as the night air brought a chill with it, a reminder that winter was just around the corner.

It doesn't matter how long it takes. I'm not going to give up, Ramona told herself. I know mother wants me to get married and start a family, but I don't care if I die an old spinster, as long as I can sing and dance, and people love me and applaud me, that's all I really want from life. She heaved in a deep breath of the fresh New York evening air.

She told herself that next time it wouldn't just be an audition. Next time the director would really see her. He wouldn't be able to take his eyes off her. She'd show him how good she could be. Then he'd choose her. Then she'd be a Broadway star, just like her father had said. She picked up her pace as she made her way home to Washington Street in the West Village, eager to tell her mother all about the statue's unveiling and her audition. When she reached their building, she saw her best friend Elizabeth arriving from the other direction. Elizabeth was heading inside with a bag of groceries tucked under one arm. Ramona guessed she was on her way home from the hotel where she worked with Ramona's mother. They usually walked home together.

"Elizabeth!" called Ramona, waving wildly at her and running up to greet her.

The two girls hugged, and Elizabeth begged, "Tell me all about it. How did it go? Did you get the part?"

Ramona glanced at her feet, twirling one foot around in place on her tip-toe.

"No, I didn't get it."

"Oh." Elizabeth's face dropped.

"It's okay though, because he said I should come back next year. So, that's positive, I think."

Elizabeth smiled again. "Yes, of course. That's great news. And, it gives you another whole year to get ready."

"Exactly!" said Ramona.

"You going in?" asked Elizabeth, propping the door

to the building open with one foot as she rearranged the grocery bag onto her hip.

"Yes. I have to help mother with a load of ironing tonight for the hotel. They make her bring it home with her on Sundays because there's just so much of it she can't possibly finish it during her shift. Do you know where she is?"

"No. Actually, I didn't see her at all today. It doesn't seem fair that she has to bring all of that laundry home," frowned Elizabeth as she slipped through the doorway.

Ramona closed the door behind them, and followed Elizabeth up the stone stairwell.

"It's not. But we need the money. Mother can't afford to lose this job, so she just does whatever they ask her to. I wish I could whisk her away from it all, like in a fairy tale or something, you know?"

"Hmm yes, if only we could all live in fairy tales."

"Although, I'm not sure I'd like to end up sleeping for a thousand years, or having someone feed me a poisoned apple." Ramona shivered.

"Very true," said Elizabeth, and the two girls laughed together.

"Speaking of fairy tales and romance, how's Arthur?" asked Ramona, raising her eyebrows.

Elizabeth blushed, and smiled shyly. "He's well. You know he graduated from college last month, and he found a job over at Lowell and Sparks. He's going to be an Associate Attorney. He says we can get married next year, once he's saved enough for a place of our own."

"That's great news," said Ramona, hugging her friend. They soon reached the third floor, where both of the girls lived directly across the hall from each other. Ramona unlocked the front door to her apartment.

"Mother!" she called, flying through the doorway. Elizabeth followed sedately behind.

The apartment was dark and cold. No fire was lit and there wasn't any food warming on the stove. The curtains lay still beside open windows, through which the frosty night air was gently blowing. The apartment looked empty, and everything was in its place. Everything except a note, a square of white on the dark timber table. Ramona hurried over to it, dropping her satchel on the floor with a bang.

Dear Ramona,

The last few years have been awful hard for me here. All alone, without your father or anyone to help me. I've done the best I could to be a mother to you, but you're grown now and don't need me any longer. You have your own life to live, and so I've decided to live mine.

I met a man. I know this will be difficult for you to understand. It was difficult for me to tell you. I couldn't face you, knowing how you'd react, but there it is. I've met someone. He has a steady job, and is a kind man, and we're getting married. He doesn't want children, and so I told him I didn't have any. It doesn't matter that you're grown, he doesn't want extra mouths to feed. So, you'll have to learn to take care of yourself now.

You're a good girl, and I love you. I hope we will see each other again someday. I'm sorry I couldn't leave you any money to live by. I don't have any to speak of, but maybe Mr. Mason will let you stay on in the apartment for a while, at least until you find a job. You can ask at the hotel, seeing as how I've left my job there—maybe they'll give it to you.

I hope all your dreams come true. Who knows, perhaps one day I'll hear about you performing on Broadway.

I'll be in living in Austin, Texas. It's a growing town according to Art. That's his name—Art Franklin. I'm going to be Mrs. Art Franklin. Doesn't that sound strange? He works at the new University of Texas there, as a history professor. We're going to live in a nice little cottage with a white picket fence. It's the kind of life I've always dreamed of so I know you'll be happy for me.

All my love,
Mother

"Who's the letter from?" asked Elizabeth.

Ramona let the letter fall to the ground. It drifted slowly, in a lilting waltz to the aged floor boards. She's getting married? What would Papa think?

It had been five years since her father had taken his own life. Ramona shook her head. She still remembered that day—there was a clear blue summer sky and a cool breeze bringing temporary relief from the stifling humidity. Ramona had come home to find her mother, Maria, wailing and screaming as she tore at her own clothes.

"Your papa has left us!" Maria had cried before dropping to her knees and burying her head in her hands.

Ramona was fourteen at the time. Old enough to understand what had happened. Even so, she never could figure why he'd done it. Her father had been addicted to gambling. His debt with the local bookkeeper had grown and grown. He became distant and easily angered by Ramona and her mother. Then, he lost his job, and try as he might, had not been able to find another one for three long months. The burden of it had become too much for him to bear. He left Maria and Ramona all alone in the world, with nothing to their names but a slew of bad debts and a lease on a shoddy, broken down apartment in the Village.

Despite all this, Ramona still remembered her papa as a kind man. A flawed man, but one who was full of love and encouragement for Ramona. She felt a haze of dizziness and nausea come over her. She fell to her hands and knees on the floor as deep sobs racked her body.

How could Mother consider marrying again without me there, standing beside her? How could she marry a man I've never even met, and leave me here all alone?

"Ramona! Ramona! What is it?" Elizabeth's voice broke through the haze that was threatening to overwhelm her.

Ramona looked up into her friend's concerned face, and stood slowly to her feet. She picked up the letter with trembling hands. Reading it over again. Maybe she could find some deeper understanding of what her mother had been thinking. Ramona knew nothing about the man her mother had run off with, other than that he was a professor from the University of Texas, and lived in Austin. Along with the note she'd left Ramona a few dollars, but no further clue as to how to contact her.

Ramona felt devastated. She stumbled to the other side of the single room apartment and sat on her bed in shock.

I'm completely alone now.

She glanced up at the door. Rent was due the following day. And their landlord, Mr. Mason, was not a kind man. He would be banging on her front door by midday if Ramona hadn't already been downstairs with a month's advance payment. Her mother had told her to ask him for some leeway in staying there, but Ramona knew that it would be a hopeless cause. Mr. Mason had thrown old Mrs. Hill out on the street only weeks earlier when her arthritis had gotten her fired at the garment factory where she worked. Ramona had tried to follow her onto the street, but the old lady had disappeared into the crowd before she got downstairs. If Mr. Mason wasn't able to find it in his heart to be lenient with that kind, old lady, Ramona knew he wouldn't help her.

She walked to the closet and pulled out her purple satin bag with the green bow. It was time to pack. And this time she would not be filling the bag with ballet shoes and a glittering stage outfit, but with everything she owned.

"Ramona! Answer me, what is going on? Are you all right?" asked Elizabeth, clutching at Ramona's arm and tugging at it in an attempt to secure her attention.

"My mother has left me," Ramona said, her chin quivering.

"What do you mean?" asked Elizabeth, letting go of Ramona's arm.

"She's gone to Texas to marry a professor. I'm all alone in the world. I have to get a job. I'll never be a Broadway star now. I have nowhere to live. I..." Ramona was babbling, and the feeling of dizziness and nausea returned as she gulped in deep breaths of cool air.

"Oh Ramona. I'm so sorry. You can stay with us. I'm

sure Mama and Papa won't mind. Honestly. Come on, let's go and ask them." Elizabeth placed her arm around Ramona's shoulders, and guided her gently toward the apartment door and into the hallway.

"What will I do now?" asked Ramona, her brown eyes wide and filled with unshed tears as she looked at Elizabeth.

"We'll figure it out. You will be fine. This is not the end of your life. It's just the beginning. You'll see." Elizabeth patted Ramona's hand, and wiped a stray tear that had trickled down her pink cheek.

"It's just the beginning."

Chapter Two

Ramona

For Ramona, time seemed to pass in a slow motion haze of activity in the weeks following her mother's departure. Sometimes she couldn't even recall what day it was, and every time Elizabeth asked her when she had last looked for a job, danced, or rehearsed, Ramona would mumble and say, "It's only been a couple of days."

"It hasn't though," Elizabeth would say.

Usually, the far more sensible Elizabeth, with her straight ash hair and plain pointed face, considered Ramona's pursuit of a life on the stage to be a foolish endeavor. She'd never said anything to discourage Ramona, but for her, being a wife and mother was all she asked of life. She had no ambition beyond that, and the way things were progressing with Arthur, it wouldn't be long until she had all that she dreamed of. For now though, Elizabeth worked as a maid in the same hotel where Ramona's mother had worked. And Elizabeth could see that the old vivacious, joyful, Ramona was drifting away. That special spark about her was fading. She had holed up in Elizabeth's bedroom, and rarely came out. So Elizabeth pressed Ramona to rehearse in an attempt to bring the girl out of the dark hole into which she had fallen.

Soon the cool air of the approaching winter was whistling down the streets and byways of the West Village, and Ramona had taken to wearing her coat everywhere she went. The leaves on the trees had changed, coating the cityscape with brilliant oranges, fiery yellows and warm brown tones. Thanksgiving was a melancholy affair for Ramona. She shared the day with Elizabeth and her family, but couldn't bring herself to be cheery in spite of their friendly banter. At the dinner that evening, the table was set with a small piece of turkey, gravy, stuffing, fresh bread rolls and several vegetable dishes. There was also soup for an appetizer, and they all waited eagerly to begin the meal while Mr. John Dresden, Elizabeth's father, said the prayer of Thanksgiving. After the prayer, he paused with a spoon full of soup just beneath the curl of his black moustache and looked at Ramona.

"So, Ramona, have you found employment yet?"

"No, not yet Mr. Dresden."

"Where have you looked?"

"I just haven't had the heart to really try anywhere yet, but I will soon. I just need a little time to think about what I should do with my life now. I always thought I'd be a performer, and now it seems that I'll have to take on some other kind of pursuit—at least until I land a role. I really don't know where to start."

"I see," he said, exchanging a look with his wife, Agatha.

"Surely they would let you take your mother's place at the hotel, dear?" questioned Agatha, taking a sip of soup.

"Actually, they've already filled that position," said Elizabeth, carefully slicing a piece of bread and laying it on her plate. She cut a portion of butter from the butter dish, and spread it thickly over the still-warm bread. It melted, running down the edges and onto the plate below.

Her parents exchanged another look, this time sharing a frown.

"Well dear, that was not very sensible—to lose such a promising lead. You know what they say, a bird in the hand is worth two in the bush."

"Oh dear, yes. You are right. I will try to be more responsible. Truly I will. I just need a little time to gather my thoughts."

"Not too long, I hope," muttered Mr. Dresden, lowering his face toward his bowl to slurp up the soup.

One day, just before Christmas, Elizabeth came home from work and called out Ramona's name. When there was no response Elizabeth entered the bedroom the two women were sharing and found Ramona curled up on her bed. Her long dark hair lay in dank and knotted braids on either side of her head, and her crumpled dress was twisted up beneath her.

"Come on," Elizabeth said, pulling Ramona up by the arms. "You're going to go and rehearse if I have to drag you down to the park to do it. This isn't like you Ramona! You've still got plenty to live for...you've got your singing and dancing, and as much as I've never understood it, I know how much it means to you. Besides, I think you ought to at least get out of the house, and maybe brush your hair."

Ramona got to her feet, smoothing out her dress and feigning a smile. "You're right," she said, nodding. "I've been feeling sorry for myself too long. Like you have said time and time again, it's not the end of the world, just the end of the life that I knew." She glanced over at her ballet shoes and, for the first time in weeks, felt the rock-like heaviness in the pit of her stomach lighten a little. "I think I'll go to rehearsal."

Elizabeth was right, Ramona thought, breathless but happy as she left the park, waving back to the girls still clustered about under a large oak tree. They waved in response, and set about removing their dance shoes and donning their coats for the walk home. Ramona pulled her coat more tightly about her body, and wrapped a knitted purple scarf around her neck against the winter chill. That's done me the world of good! Her feet sailed gracefully over the cobbled road as she made her way back home. Often, after a rehearsal she would stay and chat with her friends, but this time she couldn't wait to get back home to see Elizabeth. It was time she made a decision about what to do for money and how she could start getting back onto her own two feet. She wanted to discuss it with Elizabeth before she settled on anything.

Ramona had moved in with Elizabeth and her parents almost six weeks ago, and she knew that it was time she began to pull her weight. They had been kind enough to provide her with lodging and food, but she didn't want to live off their charity forever. Ramona brushed a stray strand of dark hair from her face, and smiled up at the darkening sky. It was a beautiful evening, full of possibility, and besides—she was in New York, where anyone could make their dreams come true if they were willing to work hard and make sacrifices.

I want Lizzie and her folks to know how much I appreciate them and everything they've done for me. They have been so kind to me. I don't know what I would have done without them.

When Ramona walked through the front door of Elizabeth's apartment that night, she found the sitting room and kitchen empty.

"Lizzie?" Ramona entered the small bedroom they shared.

Elizabeth was sitting on the bed. "Ramona, there's something I have to talk to you about. I've been speaking with my parents."

Ramona's face dropped. She sat down on the bed, beside Elizabeth, smoothing the creases in her dress and tucking one foot elegantly beneath the other.

"You can stay here for a week or two longer but after that—" Elizabeth's eyes were filled with turmoil, and her lower lip trembled as she spoke "—you'll have to find somewhere else to settle."

"Your parents don't want me staying here anymore, do they?"

Ramona sighed loudly. She knew that Elizabeth's parents had always thought that Ramona's artistic leanings and lack of supervision were a bad influence on their daughter. They refused to encourage any such outlandish behavior in their own daughter. Elizabeth's steady job as a maid earned their pride, and they looked forward to the day when she would be married to a sensible man with a solid job of his own. They saw her friendship with the untraditional Ramona as a threat to the security of Elizabeth's future.

"They say it's time you learned to take care of yourself. I'm sorry, Ramona."

Elizabeth tried to mask her dismay at having to relay this information by staring at the cracked floorboards. "It's a small apartment, Ramona. It's nothing personal against you, I promise. It's just that four people living here is such a strain on them." She managed a small smile. "But I'm sure you'll come up with a plan for what to do next. You always do."

Ramona's forced a smile across her full lips.

"It's fine, Lizzie. I promise you, I'm not worried about it at all. I'll find some way out of this. Perhaps I can get our old apartment back. I'll go and speak to Mr. Mason about it." She nodded. "Yes. I'll come up with a plan, don't you worry about me."

But Ramona couldn't come up with a plan. She had no practical skills and without the money to pay Mr. Mason there was no chance of Ramona returning to her old apartment and she knew it. Ramona watched as Elizabeth stood, straightened her skirts, and smiled down at Ramona with pity in her eyes.

She thinks I should have taken her advice and trained as a governess or a maid, not a performer. Ramona sighed. Elizabeth had told her seven years ago that she was living with her head in the clouds when the two of them were only twelve years old. Elizabeth and her parents had just moved in across the hall, and Ramona had exposed her dreams of fame and fortune to her new friend. Elizabeth hadn't approved, and for the first time in her life she believed Elizabeth had been right all along. Now that she was entirely alone in the world, how was she going to support herself with nothing but a dream to keep her warm?

Two nights later, as Ramona and Elizabeth prepared for bed, Elizabeth asked, "So, have you come up with a plan yet?"

Elizabeth's face flushed red as she fluffed her pillow, and Ramona wished she could embrace her and tell her that she didn't blame her for anything that was happening. She knew it wasn't Elizabeth's fault. Her parents didn't want Ramona to stay, and Ramona understood why. It was no one's fault, except perhaps her mother's.

Even so, thought Ramona, I don't hold it against Mother. She was lonely and afraid of spending the rest of her life on her own. She worked so hard to pay the bills, and it always seemed as though the money she earned was never quite enough to cover our expenses, especially with all of my dance and voice lessons. She wanted a better life, and I can't blame her for that. She had to leave me behind, and she knew I would manage somehow. And I will. I will figure all of this out with God's help.

In that moment Ramona felt a gentle peace filling her soul as she forgave her mother for leaving her and let go of her worry about the future.

God, please help me have wisdom to know what to do with my life. I feel so alone, I don't know where to turn. Show me the path I should take.

Time was ticking. Ramona couldn't stay in the apartment much longer. She had tried to find a job, but just before Christmas wasn't a great time to be looking for one. Though she had combed the city, there seemed to be no other places offering positions for young women such as her. But now, she had come up with a plan of sorts. It wasn't complete yet, just a partial plan really. It had been bouncing around in her head for the past few days, and she'd not been able to shake it out. Every time she tried to dismiss it to come up with something better, she couldn't, and the partial plan came creeping back into her thoughts.

Standing at the window in Elizabeth's bedroom, she stared wistfully at the street below. The trees were bare now, and their blackened trunks stood stark against a light coating of snow that had fallen across the city like a shroud in the early hours of the morning. Candlelight drifted, twinkling, out to the street from various windows in the surrounding buildings, and the sound of bells jingling merrily on sleighs passing by on the street carried up on the cold air to where she stood. Ramona reached over to the dresser beside her and picked up a hat of Elizabeth's that she'd always admired, sitting it on her head jauntily.

"I think I will go to Austin. To Texas. To find my mother."

Elizabeth stared at her with wide eyes. "But you've no idea where she is. How on earth would you find her? And how will you get to Austin? You don't have any money. Travelling on your own is so dangerous, anything could happen to you. Ramona, you ought to stay here in New York. Try again to find work, there must be something for you here."

"No, I've looked everywhere. There is no work available at the moment, not for someone with no skills or experience. Lizzie, I know that if I can just get to Texas and find Mother, everything will be all right."

Ramona tilted her head and admired the hat in the

mirror. The red band around the base of the hat worked well with her complexion, and the small feather tucked into the band looked elegant in the dim evening light.

"I'm sure that Mother only acted in haste. This man must have tricked her into it. She was distressed about the idea of losing him and being alone, that's all. She couldn't have been thinking clearly. She never would have left me like she did if she had taken some time to think it through. I know it. I'll find her, and tell her I've forgiven her and just want to be part of her life and everything will be okay again. I'm certain I will be able to find work in Austin, and surely Mother's new husband won't object to having me around now that they're married. Maybe we could even move back here to New York before spring time and everything can go back to how it was before Father died."

And I won't miss my chance to audition for Broadway next year. I won't have to give up on all of my dreams, and we can be a family again.

"Besides," Ramona said softly. "I miss her. Even if things can't return to normal, I have to at least try to find her. She is out there somewhere missing me too. I'm sure she's hoping that I'll come."

Elizabeth sighed. "And are you prepared to accept the truth, even if it turns out to be different from what you're imagining?"

Ramona took the hat off and placed it on the dark, sturdy dresser. She straightened her hair in the mirror, then turned to face Elizabeth who was examining her with a concerned look on her thin face.

"I know my mother, and I know that if I can just make my way to Texas, somehow, things will all work out. She won't be able to turn me away. And once I have the chance to explain things to her, the way that I see them, she'll understand how I feel and what's best for the two of us, and I'll be able to bring her home. She just doesn't want to be alone, but I'm going to show her that she never will be. I'll always be here for her. She doesn't have to worry about that any longer. She's all I have in the world, and I'm all she has—well me and her new husband of course—and in the end she'll see that."

Chapter Three

Michael

Michael Newhill wiped down the chestnut mare, rubbing gently where the straps of the harness had chafed at her coat. He tickled her nose and slipped a slice of carrot between her searching lips. She munched happily on the carrot, pushing against him with her whiskered nose to search for more. She nickered softly to him, and he chuckled.

"You greedy old thing," he whispered into her long ears. "That's enough carrot for today. Oh all right then, just one more."

Michael popped another long, crisp carrot between her teeth, and stepped back to watch her eat it with amusement as her nostrils flared, searching for more. He'd owned the horse, Sadie, for almost as long as he'd lived in Austin and her hair was becoming flecked with gray. He'd travelled there with a crew of construction workers from New York when he was fifteen years old after his parents told him it was time he earned his own way in life. They valued hard work, and never abided by coddling, so if he was to be a man they could be proud of, he'd have to go out and make his way in the world. He'd been the team's runner—fetching them water, food, coffee and anything else the men needed while they showed him the ropes and taught him their trade. After his apprenticeship he'd earned a reputation as a hard and skilled worker, and could take his pick of jobs around the growing town.

"Good night, Sadie," he said, patting her gently on the shoulder and stepping out of the stable. He lowered the timber bar that kept the horse inside the stable, and picked the harness up from the floor of the barn. He wiped it over with a wet cloth, and hung it up on a nail that had been driven into the stable wall high above his head. Walking through the barn, the other horses boarding there whinnied to him softly, and he smiled, then broke into a whistle. Shoving his hands deep into his pockets, he pulled the collar of his jacket up high around his neck, and moved swiftly toward Guy Town, where the men of Austin went to enjoy a drink, some entertainment, and even a haircut if that's what they were looking for.

Striding down Congress Avenue, and heading west, Michael wondered once more why he had let Tony convince him to visit the red light district. Michael could hear the noises of Guy Town drifting on the night breeze before he saw the place. The twanging of violins, the tinkle of piano keys, and the raucous laughter of saloon patrons spilled out onto the street. Lit only by the light of hanging lanterns, the streets of Austin were bathed in darkness, and the underbelly of the city was out in full force.

Turning down a side alley, Michael looked at the

handwritten signs swinging above several of the establishments announcing what lay behind the heavy timber doors. He saw his best friend Tony Campone standing outside a saloon that a sign pronounced to be "The Rusty Nail," chatting with a group of men. He strode over to them.

"Tony!"

"You made it. Michael, this is Rodney and Callum."

The men all shook hands, then headed inside the saloon.

"I can't stay long." Michael's eyes swept around the small, dark room, taking in the barber's chair in the corner where men could find their excuse for being seen in the saloon if needs be. The floor was covered in sawdust, and roughly crafted chairs were scattered about the place. A man was banging away on a small piano in one corner, and several women, in various stages of undress, loitered about the patrons, laughing and teasing them.

"Oh, come on Mike. Don't be a spoil sport. Let's have a punt. You play Faro, right?" asked Tony, heading toward a card table that was jammed up against the wall and surrounded by men.

"No, I don't. I'll watch you play," said Michael, following him reluctantly. He stood back from the card table, and leaned against the wall, crossing his ankles and tipping his black hat back from his forehead.

Tony, Rodney, and Callum all joined in the card game, and were soon making money. Michael watched with interest for a while, but before long became bored with the game and turned to scan the rest of the room. A commotion on the other side of the saloon caught his attention. A young, blonde woman was attempting to sing along with the piano and one of the patrons was grabbing at her petticoats, pulling her into his lap. She slapped his hands away good naturedly a few times, but that only made him more persistent. She stopped singing and pushed him hard, soliciting catcalls and jeers from around room. The man, obviously embarrassed, stood to his feet, his face reddening. He strode to the woman, and grabbed her hard on the arm, pulling her along after him. He was attempting to take her out the back door of the saloon, but she fought him all the way.

Michael stood up straight, watching the exchange with growing anger. He strode across the room, and flicked the man in the back of the head with his fingers.

"She doesn't want to go with you," he growled.

The man turned around, a look of surprise on his face, which soon changed to fury.

"This ain't none of your business, fella."

The man pushed out his chest and stretched himself up as tall as he could reach.

"Well, when you bother a lady like that it becomes my business," replied Michael, his hands poised beside his hips ready to react to the man's predictable attack.

Michael felt the entire room go still. The piano music stopped as the pianist turned to watch them. Soon all eyes in the saloon were trained on the two men.

"She ain't no lady," the man laughed, but his smile didn't reach his eyes.

"Well, since you aren't a gentleman, I could hardly expect you to know the difference," said Michael. A few people who were standing at the bar close to the man, moved away from him, and out of the corner of his eye Michael saw the barman grab a thick stick from behind the bar, ready to join the fray.

"Michael?" Tony had noticed what was happening, and jumped up from the card table, taking a step toward him.

Just then, the man swung at Michael. He ducked, and the punch sailed straight over his head. He jabbed a quick one-two into the man's flabby stomach, and sent him in a heap to the floor. As Michael turned to leave, two other men ran at him and were soon on top of him. A few of their flailing blows found their mark, but Michael fought them off without too much trouble. By now, the lady he had been defending had fled from the room, and several of the patrons were on their way out the door as well. Tony jumped into the fray, joining Michael as the entire saloon collapsed into an all-out brawl.

The barman tapped Michael on the shoulder, and brandished his stick with a frown. Michael nodded and made his way toward the door, intent on a quick exit with Tony right behind him. They stumbled through the doorway, and ran down the avenue, listening as the sounds of the brawl continued without them.

Puffing hard, they stopped on Main Street. Michael leaned against a wall, and rubbed his hands across his forehead, pulling his hat down low. Tony bent forward at the waist, resting his hands on his knees and breathing hard.

"What the heck, Michael?" he asked between gasps.

Michael chuckled, and they both burst into a fit of laughter. When they finally regained their breaths, Michael said, "I told you not to take me to a saloon, didn't I?"

"Yes, I guess you did. But why can't you just enjoy yourself like everyone else?"

"He was getting rough with a lady." Just thinking about it again brought a fresh frown to his face.

"So what? You don't know her."

"I don't have to know her. I just can't stand by and watch it happening without doing something about it. You should know this about me by now."

"You're right. I should have known better. No more saloons for you."

"Thank you. I just don't have the stomach for them anyway. Give me an open field or a rugged mountain side, or a crystal clear creek any day of the week over a smoky, rodent-infested saloon."

"But that's where the women are. Aren't you at least interested in meeting women?"

"No, not in a place like that. I want a wife, and I'm hardly going to find one at the Rusty Nail, am I?"

"You'll not find one in Austin, and that's a fact." Tony stood to his feet and began to make his way homeward.

"You might be right about that," said Michael with a strange look on his face.

Chapter Four

Ramona

"Look at this!" said Elizabeth, waving her hand at Ramona to beckon her back.

Ramona was walking down the stone steps of the Catholic Church that Elizabeth and her parents attended each Sunday morning for mass. Elizabeth had paused at the top of the stairs to point at something on the bulletin board just outside the church doors. A cream colored flyer flapped in the light breeze that came sailing through the city off the waters of the nearby bay. Ramona was distracted. She knew that Elizabeth's parents wouldn't allow her to stay in the apartment for much longer. She sighed loudly as she spun about on the stairs to face Elizabeth.

"What is it?"

"It's a flyer for Mail Order Brides. It says here that men out on the frontier want women from New York to marry, Ramona. Why, this could be just the thing for you!"

Ramona screwed up her nose and sniffed.

"Really, Lizzie," Ramona said. "Do you really think that I'd be a Mail Order Bride and marry some man I've never met in a dusty town in some uncivilized western settlement? How would I ever get to Broadway if I did that? No thank you. Getting married is the last thing on my mind. Once you're married, you're never your own person again. My mother always told me that. She said, 'Ramona, the moment you marry, your life is not your own,' and she'd sigh like it had been a big mistake to give up her freedom. Well, not me. I'm going to follow my dreams, not get married and have babies. You know I want to go to Texas to find Mother, and then perform on Broadway. How would getting married help me do either of those two things?"

Elizabeth closed her mouth tightly, and made her way down the stairs, careful to avoid slipping on the icy ones, meeting Ramona halfway down. Ramona glared at her, then turned to follow her home. It was all well and good for Elizabeth to suggest marrying a stranger in some distant and lawless town when she had her handsome and successful lawyer here in New York to marry. It wouldn't be Elizabeth having to go traipsing across the country to marry someone who could quite possibly be old and hideously ugly, and possibly even a criminal. Well, Ramona wasn't such a beggar that she had to do it either, and she wasn't about to turn her life upside down just because she happened to be running low on money and luck. She had dreams, and she was going to make them happen, somehow.

Trust in Me.

Ramona started, a warm tingle going up and down her spine.

Trust in Me.

Ramona's eyes filled with tears, as she hurried after Elizabeth down the frosty cobblestone avenue toward their apartment.

I trust You, God. I just don't know what to do, or where to turn. The only thing I have to hold onto are my dreams. I don't want to let go of them because without them I have nothing and no one. But I'll trust in You.

Back at home Ramona was folding her dresses and packing them into her travelling trunk. Elizabeth was sitting on the bed watching her and chewing on a fingernail, her toe tapping nervously on the timber floor.

"Mail Order Brides are so old fashioned! I'm surprised those agencies even still operate!" Ramona pursed her lips, and nodded emphatically to make her point. "Though I suppose out West things are a bit different."

Elizabeth took her finger out of her mouth and smiled grimly.

"Yes, things won't be quite so modern out west. It will take you a while to get used to life on the frontier."

Ramona whirled around to face her.

"You're not seriously suggesting I go through with this, are you?" Ramona put her hands on her hips and scowled at Elizabeth. "Why, Lizzie, can you imagine me tied to a man's arm? The arm of a man I've never even met? A man who can't find a wife where he lives, so he must be old, ugly and mean. Why, I'd sooner collapse here on the spot. No man is going to tell me how to live or what to do. Do you think a husband would let me sing and dance on the stage? Of course not. He'd want me to stay home and raise babies, that's what, and my dreams would be dead. Dead!"

Elizabeth rolled her eyes at Ramona's dramatic speech. She wasn't taken in by Ramona's hysterics this time. "Ramona," she said sternly. "You need to think sensibly about this. You can't stay here forever. Mama and Papa won't allow it. And how else are you going to support yourself?"

Ramona's mouth fell open, stunned by Elizabeth's lack of confidence in her abilities.

"Why, I'll sing, I'll dance."

"Ramona! Be realistic, please. This is serious."

Ramona stood up and flounced across the room to fetch her dancing gowns to pack into the top of the trunk. Deep down, she knew that Elizabeth was right, but she couldn't bring herself to admit it now. She knew that she needed to find a solution to her predicament, and fast. But the thought of marrying a stranger in some far off frontier town made her quake with fright. She'd never been anywhere on her own, and she'd never travelled outside of New York before. So, the idea of journeying to the other side of the country on her own to meet, marry and live with a stranger filled her with dread.

"I don't want to talk about it any longer, Elizabeth May. And—" Ramona's voice broke as tears filled her eyes "—I can't bear the thought of leaving you—my only friend in this whole wide world. Please don't make me go."

Elizabeth ran to her friend and flung her arms around Ramona's neck, stroking her back gently.

"Oh Ramona, my dear, I don't want you to leave either. But what will you do?"

"I don't know. But I do know this, God will provide a way forward. I just have to trust Him."

* * *

The following day, Ramona woke early and lay still in her bed without moving. She stared at the peeling paint on the ceiling above her head and thought long and hard about the future. What was she going to do? She had pounded the pavement looking for employment ever since the Dresdens had given her notice, but there was none to be had. And she knew that in a few days' time, she would be homeless. Christmas had come and gone, and now a bleak and icy January was well underway. She'd already stayed well past her welcome at Elizabeth's place. It was time for Ramona to grow up and make some decisions about where her life was headed. It was time for her to do something, to take back the life that she had lost and to go after what she wanted.

When Elizabeth awoke, Ramona was already up and dressed. Her hair was combed back into a tight bun, and her face shone from being scrubbed clean.

"What is it?" asked Elizabeth, rubbing her eyes as she sat up in bed.

"I'm going to do it," said Ramona.

"Do what?" asked Elizabeth, yawning widely.

"Get married. I'm going to be a Mail Order Bride."

"What?" Elizabeth was suddenly wide awake, and threw the covers back, leaping to her feet.

"Yes. I'm getting married. I bet that Mail Order Bride service has men down there in Austin. I'm going to get one of those men to pay for me to travel to Austin, and then I'm going to find Mother."

"Ramona! You wouldn't. They would be expecting you to marry them. You can't lie, and that's what it would be. It would be dishonest to have them pay your way to Austin only to leave them at the altar to go and find your mother. It just wouldn't be right."

Elizabeth's face flushed red, and she stamped one foot in indignation as she spoke.

"I don't care, Elizabeth. I have to do something, and I've decided that this is it. God has provided a way for me to get to Texas to find Mother, and I'm going to take it. I know it's dishonest, and I don't want to lie or hurt anyone, I really don't. I promise you—if there were some other way to get to Austin, I'd do it. But I can't think of any other way. Can you?"

Elizabeth slumped back onto the bed and shook her head slowly. "No, I can't."

"So you see—I have to do it. I'm sure the man who I'm to marry will get over it quickly and find himself someone else to marry. He isn't in the same kind of predicament that I am. He's likely to be settled, and have a steady income, or he wouldn't be looking for a wife and family. He'll be disappointed of course, but he'll soon move on and find someone else. And I will have found Mother and everything will work out just fine, I know it will. God told me to trust Him when you found that flyer for the Mail Order Bride service, and I believe He wants me to do this. Otherwise, I just don't know what I'll do."

She knelt in front of Elizabeth, and took her hands, gazing at her with pleading eyes.

"All right Ramona. I'll help you to do it. You're right—it may be the only way you get to see your mother again. Let's go down to the Mail Order office today. I plucked one of the flyers from the bulletin board and have it right here in my dresser drawer."

Elizabeth stood to her feet and walked to the dresser.

Opening one of the drawers, she withdrew a crumpled flyer and handed it to Ramona who smoothed it out to read over again.

"Thank you, Lizzie. I know I don't need your approval, but I'd like to have it just the same. I never had a sister, but I believe you're the closest thing to a sister a girl could ever ask for. I wish you could come with me. It's going to be awful lonesome taking this journey without you. Promise me you'll write?"

"Of course I will. Just as soon as you write to let me know where you are, I'll write back to you the very same day, I promise. You're the sister I always wanted as well. I just hope that we'll see each other again someday."

The two women embraced with tears streaking their forlorn faces. Their lives were about to change forever, and neither one of them could imagine what the future might hold for them. After breakfast Ramona walked through the city to the address on the flyer with Elizabeth by her side. They found the office of the Mail Order Bride service in a run-down building on the other side of Central Park. After waiting in the reception area for a few minutes, an attractive middle-aged woman with dark hair piled high on her head strode into the room and called Ramona's name. The woman was in charge of the agency. Her name was Rachel Moore, and Ramona followed her back to a small office with frosted glass windows. Elizabeth stayed seated in the reception area, her foot tapping nervously against the tiled floor, one finger held up to her mouth as she chewed on a nail.

Rachel Moore, a kind but stern woman, looked Ramona up and down with a careful eye and offered her a high-backed wooden chair. Rachel walked around to the other side of her desk and sat behind it, pulling a ledger from a drawer of the desk, and laying it down on top of the desk. After a brief interview, Rachel walked Ramona through the entire Mail Order Bride process. She told her that each prospective husband was interviewed, thoroughly checked out, and would pay to have her travel out to marry him. While she spoke, she flicked through a ledger, her finger drifting across the page before turning it over and moving onto the next page of the folder.

Ramona studied the floor, her eyes flicking between her hands and Rachel's face as she asked the question that had been on her mind ever since she'd heard about the scheme.

"Are any of the men from Austin, Texas?"

Rachel adjusted the spectacles on her nose and glanced down the list. A crease appeared on her fair forehead, and she rubbed it vigorously with her fingertips.

"Hmmm, let me see. Yes, there are, actually." She placed the folder down with a thud. "One might be suitable for you. His name is Michael Newhill. He's a construction worker."

Ramona drew in a sharp breath. She clasped her hands together. "Oh yes, surely we're a match, Miss Moore? Please—can you check? It's just that I've heard so much about Austin. It sounds like a fascinating town, and I'd really love to go somewhere interesting. So many places on the frontier sound so dull, or even dangerous. If I could go to Austin I just know I'd be happy there. Do you think this Michael Newhill might be a good match for me?"

Rachel sat still, watching Ramona's face closely as she made her appeal.

"Well my dear, I'm sure you are a good match. Let's see. Yes, I think that would work out just fine. He looks like he is a decent man, with a solid income and good prospects. You would do well to be married to such a man. Yes, I think that would work out well. If you are happy to proceed, I'll write to Mr. Newhill and let him know your position. He will wire us the money for you to travel to Austin, and will meet the coach there. Well now, that was easy enough. It usually takes a lot longer to find an appropriate match for a young woman like yourself, Ramona. You have made my job a sight easier today. Well now, I do believe you will be happy with Mr. Newhill. What a pleasure it is for me to help two people find love."

Rachel slammed the register closed, and removed her spectacles to rub her eyes.

"How long do you think it will be before I hear from Mr. Newhill?" asked Ramona, leaning forward in her chair, her brown eyes wide.

"I will wire him in Austin, and if he wires back directly it should only be a few days at most." Rachel reached for her quill and made notes on a notepad in front of her.

"Thank you so much for your help," said Ramona, standing to her feet. "I guess this means that I'll be heading to Austin by the end of the week then."

"You surely could be if everything goes well."

Ramona sighed, and smoothed her hair back from her forehead with both hands.

"Austin. It's so far away. Such a strange, unknown place. I never thought I'd be going there in my life, and certainly not on my own to meet a stranger who I'm to marry."

She stared down wistfully at her empty left ring finger. Even though she had no intention of marrying Mr. Newhill, she found herself wondering what kind of man he might be, and what it would feel like to be married. She shook her head. Marrying was not a part of her plan. She was going to Austin to find her mother, and then she was on a bearing for Broadway. She would sing and dance, and one day she'd be a star, and then everyone would see how special she truly was. Nothing was going to stand in her way.

Chapter Five

Michael

Michael paused to wipe the sweat off his brow. Working construction at the site of the new State Capitol building, even during winter, was hard going. There was no shelter or shade from the sun or the wind, and the days were long and harsh. Since the end of the civil war Austin had boomed, and its growth came on the backs of men like Michael. He stood to his feet, wiping the last of the mortar from his trowel as the final brick for that line of wall he was working on stood evenly in its place. He stretched his arms skyward, working out the kinks in his back that had camped just above his waist after stooping for so long over the growing wall. He glanced toward the supervisor's tent and noticed the foreman glaring at him over a clipboard, his spectacles hanging low near the pointy tip of his nose, a line of sweat beading across his balding forehead.

"Hiya buddy." Tony came up behind him and slapped him on the back. He exclaimed, "Don't tell me you're tired already, you slacker! We've still got eight hours of work ahead of us. You're going to get on ol' four-eyes' bad side if you're not careful. And you know what happens when you're on his bad side? You have to listen to his whiny voice telling you off for at least a full ten minutes."

"Don't I know it," Michael said. They both chuckled, and Michael hurried toward the wheelbarrow where he mixed up another batch of mortar. Tony followed him, and helped by adding water to the mixture as Michael blended it with a square-nosed shovel. He smiled at Tony. Michael was in high spirits today, regardless of the workload. "It's all worth it. I need the money, because tomorrow..."

"I know, I know," Tony said. His own smile faded, and he took on a look of irritation. "Ramona's arriving. You haven't stopped talking about it for days." Tony shook his head. "I was hoping you'd come to your senses and have changed your mind by now. Why do you wanna go and get married anyway? There's plenty of women around here for a man who wants to be single and enjoy the finer things in life. We work hard, we play hard. It's the life men all over the world can only dream of. Why would you wanna go and change that on me? I just don't understand you at all sometimes."

"You know I want a family. It's all right for you—your entire extended family live here in Austin. But I'm on my own here, and it's awful lonely when I go home at night. I've always wanted someone to come home to, and the timing is right. I've got a good job, I've saved and bought a nice house, and I'm ready. There aren't a lot of good women around here, Tony, not of the marrying kind. Every woman I meet is either unsuitable or already married. I mean, you tell me, when was the last time you met a single woman you'd take home to meet your mother?"

Tony kicked the ground with the toe of his boot, a light flush creeping across his tanned cheeks.

"Meet my Mamma? Heck no. I don't bring any of them home to meet her. That would be asking for trouble."

"Exactly my point. Austin's a real nice place to live. It's got potential, it's gonna be somethin'. I don't wanna move, but if I'm to have the family I've always wanted, I either have to leave here, or have a wife sent to me." He paused and looked around the half-finished building before adding, "I mean look at this place. This building's gonna be amazing, you just wait and see. It feels good to be part of somethin' big like this, it sure does."

Tony kept mixing. "I understand you wantin' a family. But there ain't no reason for you to rush into it. You're young. Only twenty-five. There's plenty of time to have a family. We should enjoy our freedom for as long as we can. Once we're old and tired we can tie on the ball and chain." He chuckled at his own joke and leaned on his shovel, sweat beads glimmering on his dark brow. "I know one thing for sure, you don't need to order a bride in the mail. Especially not one from New York. Who knows what you'll get? Do you really think a New York gal is going to fit in down here in Austin? Do you think she's gonna take to you? Heaven only knows what she'll be like."

Michael turned back to the wheelbarrow to continue mixing.

"That's right. Heaven knows. I've prayed about this, and I trust God to bring me a wife who will suit me, and will be my partner in life, whether she comes by mail or some other way."

Tony sighed with exasperation. "You and your God," he said. "Well, don't come cryin' to me when it all falls apart, and it will, you mark my words. I just wish you'd take some more time to think it through first."

"I don't want to waste any more time. We'll be working on this site for at least another two years Tony, and even then I don't know that I'll want to uproot and head north, and I don't want to wait any longer to be part of a family. I want someone by my side to share my life with. A good, sensible wife. I don't know what Ramona will be like either, but I'm willing to give her a shot. God will take care of the rest."

Tony scoffed. "Well, fine. I'll let it go and I won't raise the subject again. But, just one more thing—have you thought about the fact that you just can't seem to talk to women at all? How's that gonna work?"

Tony chortled as he began slipping bricks into place and slapping mortar underneath and between each one, his hands flying back and forth along the line.

Michael's face reddened. "I can talk to them." He threw the shovel to the ground, and joined Tony, the two men laying bricks smoothly and efficiently together in a row.

Tony raised his eyebrows. "Can you? You start quivering as soon as you get within a foot of a woman!"

Michael reached a hand up to comb it through the brown hair that had a habit of falling across his tanned face. "Well, this will make things easy for me, won't it? She's already agreed to marry me, that's the hard part out of the way. I think this is going to work out just fine. There's none of that awkwardness that comes between me and any woman when I like her, but I can't seem to find the words to tell her how I feel, or to ask her if she'd like to take a stroll with me, or sit by me in church. That's all out of the way. We're getting married, so of course she's going to be sitting by me, and walking with me. This way will be so much easier."

Tony's laughter filled the construction site. He slapped his thigh as his peals of mirth rang out, echoing off the mounds of dirt and bricks surrounding them. The foreman spun about to glare at the two of them once more.

"Ah Michael—you poor sod. That shows how much you know about marriage," he said, wiping the tears from his eyes.

Chapter Six

Ramona

"Are you sure about this?" Elizabeth asked as she gingerly stepped onto the thick boards lining the train platform. It shook beneath their feet. The train was already approaching. "You've never even seen a picture of Mr. Newhill."

The girls were standing in the middle of an immense building, its glass ceiling was shaped like a dome that sparkled high above their heads. In front of them a dozen raised platforms peopled by smartly dressed passengers lay in bright, clean rows over the ground. The sun shone down brilliantly through the glass above, sending kaleidoscope colors dancing across the train carriages as they moved deftly in and out of the station.

"You're the one who talked me into this Mail Order scheme in the first place!" Ramona said, astonished that Elizabeth could be having second thoughts now.

"I know." Elizabeth stared down at the polished oak beneath her feet. "But I did mean for you to pick a man based on your compatibility, not based solely on his location."

As the two women spoke, the sparkling carriages of an engine-less steam train glided quietly into the station, braking gently to stop in front of them at the platform.

"Wow!" said Elizabeth, "would you look at that? I can't believe I've never caught a train from the Grand Union Depot before. I mean, I've been down here to look around of course, everyone has, but I've never actually caught one of the trains anywhere. It's sad really, I've never been anywhere at all."

"Me either," said Ramona, staring at the silent carriage standing only feet away from her. She shivered as a rush of nervous energy sent a jolt through her body.

"Excuse me?" Ramona hailed a porter. "This luggage is to go onto the train please."

"Yes ma'am." The porter tipped his hat, and reached for Ramona's bags, deftly swinging them onto the train carriage one by one. He slipped into the carriage after them and carried the bags out of sight, returning to the platform a few moments later. He was about to move on when Ramona stopped him again.

"One last thing if you please, where is the locomotive for this train?"

He chuckled, and wiped the sweat from his brow with a handkerchief.

"Mr. Vanderbilt didn't want any smoke clouding up his glass ceiling, so the engines have to disengage before they arrive at the depot and switch over to a line that runs along the side of the depot. The trains glide in, and the brakeman stops it at the platform. Then, the engine trundles back around to pull the carriages out from the other end. It's somethin', ain't it?"

"Well, I never," exclaimed Elizabeth.

"Will that be all, ma'am?" asked the porter.

"Yes, thank you."

Ramona pulled her travelling gloves onto her hands, pushing the fingers securely in place one by one. She rearranged several of the pins that were securing her hat over her tightly coiled bun, tears filling her eyes as she avoided Elizabeth's face.

"I suppose this is it?" she said, finally looking up to meet Elizabeth's gaze.

Elizabeth's cheeks were wet and she dabbed beneath her eyes with a handkerchief before blowing her nose zealously. She let out a heavy sigh. "I can't believe you're really going, Mona. When will I see you again?"

Ramona pushed a smile firmly across her countenance and reached out to embrace her oldest friend.

"I won't be gone forever, in fact I plan on returning within the year so that I can get back to auditioning," she reassured her. "I want you to know that I appreciate everything you've done for me." She took Elizabeth's hand in hers. "You've been a good friend to me when I needed it the most. I won't ever forget that."

It took almost two days for the train to make its way to Albany, Texas. From there Ramona disembarked to catch a stagecoach the rest of the way to Austin. She was restless for the duration of the journey. The auditions she was missing in New York weighed heavily on her mind, as she thought about the girls she knew so well from years of training and auditioning together who would be winning the roles she so desperately wanted.

But most importantly, she wanted to find her mother and she didn't know how she could even begin that search, having no money or transportation in Austin.

What if Mother has already left Austin? What if I can't find her—what will I do then? What if I do find her, but she truly never wants to see me again and turns me away?

When the train finally pulled into the station at Albany in the early morning hours of the second day, Ramona was relieved to feel solid ground beneath her feet again. She stepped from the train onto the dusty, worn platform and her eyes widened as she took in the half-finished town. People rushed to and fro along the streets, and everything seemed to be covered in a sheen of brownish orange that floated through the air, and was whipped about in flurries by the wind. It was very different from New York City and everything Ramona had ever known, but it did have a tinge of excitement and newness about it.

Not much glamor out here. In that moment she almost wanted to run after the train, to scream out to the conductor to stop, and take her back to New York City. Instead, she squared her shoulders and looked for the coach.

"Stagecoach, ma'am?" asked a weathered looking man.

"Yes, to Austin please."

"Name?"

"Ramona Selmer."

"Yes ma'am, your passage has been paid for through to Austin."

He picked up her bags, one in each hand, "This way please."

Well, that was easy enough.

Ramona followed him to the stagecoach where the fresh horses were stamping their feet and snorting steam into the cool morning air, eager to get going. The driver secured her luggage to the top of the coach, and then opened the door for her to enter. She stepped up and into the coach, happy to discover the seat to be quite comfortable and only one other passenger on board.

Even though the distance between Albany and Austin was much shorter than from New York to Albany, this part of the journey was by far the longest and most difficult. They travelled for four days, stopping at a different boarding house each night for food and rest. In the morning they ate a hearty breakfast, and the cook packed them a picnic lunch to eat on the road. Then they were off again. By the time they reached Austin, Ramona felt as though her teeth had almost been jolted from her head, the sounds of horse hooves thundering along the ground now a permanent fixture in her brain. Her eyes were full of dust, her mouth was constantly dry, and her clothing was limp, dirty and soaked through with her sweat. The fresh winter air had been left behind, and seemed to be reserved only for nighttime in Texas. The days were hot and dry, and the air filling the coach was thick with dust.

It was evening when they finally arrived in Austin. Ramona staggered from the coach. Her legs turned to jelly, and she fell flat on her face in the dusty street. She sat still on the road with her dress bunched up around her, tears filling her eyes.

What a great impression I'm going to make on my prospective groom. Although, since I have no intention of actually going through with the wedding, I suppose it doesn't really matter what he thinks of me.

The driver set her luggage down on the sidewalk and rushed to help her to her feet.

"Don't worry Ma'am, happens all the time. Takes a while to get used to travelling by coach over those kinds of distances."

"Thank you. You are very kind."

In minutes, the driver and his coach were gone. Headed no doubt for a boarding house where they would spend the night before starting their journey all over again the next day. Ramona sighed and sat down on top of her purple satin bag with the green bows. As she sat there, she watched the townsfolk rushing by, or stopping to chat, the streets almost empty as people made their way home for supper.

I wonder what Mr. Newhill will look like. How am I to recognize him? I do hope he has remembered me. Everyone around me looks so keenly focused. They each have a purpose, something they must do, and they are intent on doing it. It feels very strange to have nothing at all to do but sit here, in the dust, waiting for someone who may or may not show up. And if he doesn't, what then?

Ramona straightened her back. She had to remember: she had a purpose as well. To find her mother. That's what mattered. Once she had located her mother, everything would be okay. They would be together again, as a family, and she wouldn't have to worry about what she might eat or how she could get back to New York. Mother would take care of everything.

"Ramona?" A quiet, deep voice interrupted her thoughts.

Ramona jumped, startled.

"Yes?" she asked, thinking that the young man before her with the sandy blonde hair and large green eyes must be from the coach service and had come to collect her bags to take to the boarding house. Although his clothes and boots were caked with mud, Ramona couldn't help but notice his chiseled features and the two large dimples in his tanned cheeks beneath striking green eyes.

"Can I take this for you?" He nodded at her luggage, his black hat twisting around in his hands.

Ramona nodded. "Thank you. I'm actually waiting for someone. Do you know a Michael Newhill?" she asked absentmindedly, standing on tiptoes to search the length of the street. "He was supposed to meet me here."

The young man fumbled with the suitcase. "I'm, I'm Michael," he said quietly, as though he was almost unsure of the fact himself.

Ramona's eyes widened. "Oh. Of course. I'm sorry—I'm Ramona Selmer. It's a pleasure to meet you, Mr. Newhill."

Michael sat the bag back down and reached for her hand. Ramona looked at his brown hand as it took her own in a firm grasp. "I figured as much. Pleased to meet you, Ramona."

She felt a blush creeping up her neck.

Why am I blushing? He's good looking that's for certain, but it doesn't matter one jot since I'm not marrying him.

"Thank you," she said hurriedly.

She squinted up at the man and considered his appearance. Yes, she decided. He is kind looking. Handsome too, if he were to wash up a little and polish those boots of his. She shook her head and her curls bounced. But none of that is of concern anyway. It doesn't matter what he looks like. It doesn't matter if he is kind. All that matters is that I find Mother as soon as possible.

Michael seemed to perk up. "You look as though you could do with something to eat and a wash after that long journey."

Ramona's mouth opened to shoot back a retort, but she thought better of it and closed it again.

Michael noticed the scowl forming on Ramona's face.

"I mean, you look real pretty. It's just that I've taken that stagecoach journey before, and I know how it feels to get to the end of the ride, that's all."

Ramona beamed. "Thank you, Michael. That's awful sweet of you to say. Of course, I would love some food and a place to wash up."

Michael grinned shyly and reached for her bags. Picking them up he made his way over to an open wagon that was sitting behind a beautiful old chestnut mare.

"Then, maybe tomorrow you could show me around Austin? I'm keen to see all the sights." Ramona glanced up and down the street before following Michael to the wagon. "I'm in quite a hurry to see all the sights, actually."

Chapter Seven

Michael

Michael kept sneaking sidelong glances at the woman sitting next to him in the wagon. He still couldn't believe she was here. To Michael, Ramona—with her exotic mountain of curls and huge brown eyes—looked just like the glamorous women he'd seen on stage at the Austin Theater. He'd been to see a show with Tony and one of his many beaus the previous year. Ramona looked like she should be on stage, not marrying someone like him. She was sitting so close to him in the wagon Michael was becoming even more nervous with each passing moment. He pondered over what he could say to her to break the awkward silence that had descended between them, but even when he finally thought of something his throat seemed to constrict and he couldn't speak.

Luckily for him, Ramona was both talkative, and seemingly oblivious to how nervous he was. She broke the silence between them happily, and filled the night air with her silken voice. Her chatter helped him to relax a little as he guided the horse and wagon around town and home to his newly built little house. In the weeks since he had first decided to find a bride, Michael had purchased a new home, built by one of Tony's cousins. It was small but quaint and in a good neighborhood that was filling up with similar newly built houses. Ramona nattered happily about her trip to Austin, and then moved on, telling Michael all about her dreams of singing and dancing on Broadway.

"I've been dancing since I was four years old," she said, craning her neck to take in her surroundings in the dark city. "It's always been my dream to sing and dance on stage."

She sounds a little sad.

Michael slapped Sadie with the reins, and she jumped forward into a quick trot.

"Austin is quite a modern town, really," Michael said quietly. "There are a lot of artistic types here. I think you'll fit in just fine," he said.

Ramona paused for a second before she nodded her head quickly and smiled brightly. "Perhaps."

They navigated their way through the construction site of the capitol building where Michael worked. He pointed out the area where he was currently working, and told her a little about his job. He told her about the foreman, and about Tony.

"Tony's always been there for me, since I don't have any family in these parts. He's Italian too, you know? Like you."

"Oh?" she said. "I look forward to meeting him. You'll have to introduce us soon," Ramona said.

Then, furrowing her brow a little she added, "Michael, you don't know anyone who works at the University of Texas, do you?"

Michael shook his head as the wagon left the construction site and headed toward the neighborhood where Michael's small house sat perched on a crest. "No, sorry," he said. "I don't know anyone in those circles."

"Oh," Ramona said, leaning back against the seat. Michael heard the disappointment in her voice.

"Why do you ask?"

"No reason," Ramona said quickly. "I was just curious, that's all. Never mind."

"I can take you up there if you like," Michael said, keen to see her smile again. "We can go look at the university together. I've never been, really, but I know there's nice parks on the grounds, with fountains and places to sit. We could sit, have a little picnic."

Ramona nodded her head. "That sounds nice," she said, leaning her head back against the leather seat. "Right now, all I know is that I'm awful tired after my trip. Let's do it soon though."

"You got it."

"Michael, where are we going?"

"Uh. Oh, sorry. I should have told you. Back to my house."

"Oh!"

"I mean, not just us—Fred and Mary will be there too. They're friends of mine. They've agreed to stay with us until the wedding."

Ramona shifted in her seat, and coughed loudly, covering her mouth with her gloved hand.

Michael frowned. "I thought about putting you up at

a hotel, but then decided you might be more comfortable at the house. 'Course if you'd rather…"

"No, no. That sounds fine. Really, please don't trouble yourself. I'm sure it will be wonderful."

They rode the rest of the way in silence, Michael was too nervous to broach the topic of the wedding again. When he'd mentioned it, she had jumped in place, as though a bolt of lightning had gone straight through her. There's something on her mind. And I don't know what it is. Maybe she is just tired after all, like she said. Michael gripped the reins tightly as he steered the wagon home.

Now that she's seen Austin, and seen me, it's likely she won't want to go through with it anyway. I wonder what a girl like Ramona is doing travelling across the country on her own to marry a stranger. A woman like her, so beautiful and glamorous. She likely took one good look at me and realized she'd made a huge mistake.

He turned to observe the girl curled up on the wagon seat beside him, her large brown eyes already drooping closed, her head lolling to one side.

I saw the disappointment on her face when I told her I don't know any university types. A girl like her, she must be used to spending time with intellectuals and performers. I'll likely never be enough for her.

When they arrived at the house, Ramona shook the sleepiness from her limbs, and clambered out of the wagon on Michael's arm. The cottage was very cozy looking, and a soft light drifted from the front windows and across the newly graveled garden path that led to a sturdy front door. Michael grabbed Ramona's luggage and helped her inside. A man and a woman seated before a roaring fire jumped to their feet and hurried over to meet them.

"Ramona, this here is Mary, and her husband Fred."

"How do you do?" Ramona greeted them with a curtsey, and the two women shook hands.

"They're goin' to be stayin' here with us, 'til the wedding."

"Oh, of course. How lovely, it will be so much fun—all bunking together." Ramona smiled warmly at the couple, who beamed back at her.

"We're so pleased to meet you, Ramona. You just make yourself at home here, we'll stay out of your way. This is your home now, and you're mighty welcome in it," said Mary, grasping Ramona's hand once more, her bright eyes twinkling.

"Thank you, Mary."

"Come now, I'll show you to your room," said Michael, leading the way.

As he showed her to the spare bedroom, Michael made a vow to himself not to give up on her too quickly. Perhaps I can prove that I am good enough to be her husband, he thought, showing Ramona to her bedroom as he placed her satin bag down at the base of the four poster bed.

"She's all set then?" Mary appeared behind Michael and followed him out of Ramona's room and down the hall.

"Yes. And I really want to thank you and Fred for staying here with us."

"You're very welcome."

"Nothin' to it Mike, we're delighted to do it." Fred was seated in the living room back in front of the fire reading a book.

"The house is lovely, by the way," said Mary, sitting down beside Fred on a wooden chair that Michael had whittled from a leftover piece of oak.

"Thank you kindly. I'm very happy with it. I just hope Ramona will be content here too."

"Of course she will be. What more could any woman want?" Mary smiled warmly at him, and picked up a half-finished shawl she was knitting.

Michael snuck down the hallway five minutes later to say good night to Ramona and to see if she needed anything else, but Ramona had already fallen to sleep. The rhythmic sound of her breathing drifted out to him through the open door, and he pulled it closed behind him with a smile. As he strode toward his own bedroom, he couldn't help wondering what the future might be like, and hoped that his days of loneliness were finally over.

The next morning, Michael was summoned to the front door by a loud knocking. Then Tony's voice bellowed loudly through the house. "Michael! Come on. We're going to be late for work."

Michael hurried to the door, pulling on his boots as he went.

"Shhh," he said. "Ramona's sleeping. She's exhausted. I'm running late 'cause I was creeping around, trying to be real quiet so as not to wake her."

Tony shook his head and tutted.

Walking to the construction site, Tony had plenty to say. "She's already got you under her spell. I hope you ain't gonna make a habit of being late. I see she's the sort of princess type that likes to lay around all day long. I won't say I told you so, but."

"Go easy, Tony. It's only her first morning after a long trip."

"So, she's not a princess then?"

Michael paused before he spoke.

"She wears her hair in this real modern style," Michael commented. "People around here might think it's too modern." In fact he was worried they would think Ramona was too modern, all round.

"I told you so," Tony said pointedly. "Those New York women, they ain't got no place around here." He lowered his voice. "And she's foreign on top of all that, ain't she?"

"Italian parents." Michael rolled his eyes. "Like you, Tony. She was born and raised in New York. But none of that matters a jot to me anyhow."

"I'll say it again. You should wait for a good old-fashioned pioneering woman. Someone used to the frontier life. That's what I'm fixin' to do. It won't be long before this town is crawling with women. And a handsome man like yourself ain't gonna have any trouble finding a sweet, practical woman to marry. You don't need a fancy New York type. She'll be of no earthly use at all. Mark my words."

Michael didn't want to admit it, but he was starting to think that Tony had a valid point. He wasn't sure Ramona would ever really fit here. He couldn't imagine her raising babies, washing laundry, baking and doing all the things that a pioneer woman had to do just to get by each day. It was a grueling life, and Ramona didn't look as though she knew much about hard work. Michael had never met a woman like her before. Not in Texas, anyway. Maybe that's how they all are in New

York City, but around here she is going to stand out like a sore thumb.

Not that Michael hadn't already noticed the way that the other men in town stopped and stared when Ramona passed by. As they rode home in the wagon the previous evening, men had paused in the street, taken their hats off and stared.

He pondered the situation all day long while they worked in the heat of the Texas sun. Walking home that evening, he wondered whether he should just ask her outright what she planned on doing.

I'll talk to her tonight. I need to find out why Ramona came to Texas, and if she still intends to become my wife. I need to find out if she really means to marry me.

Chapter Eight

Ramona

When Ramona awoke the next morning, it took her a moment to remember where she was. Looking around the room, it all came rushing back to her. She was at Michael's house, in Austin, Texas. The morning light poured through the window, already bringing with it the promise of a warm winter's day. The bed she lay in looked as though it had been hewn by hand from a thick log, wooden nails held each piece in place. The straw tick rustled beneath her, and she could smell the freshly dried grasses through the linens. A hand-whittled rocker sat beside the bed, with an extra crocheted blanket spread over one arm. A rustic vase, made of clay and filled with fresh flowers, sat gaily on a small table against the wall. Ramona sighed with pleasure. The room really was very homely. She tried to remember what the rest of the house had looked like, but it had been so late when she'd arrived the previous night and she'd been so exhausted, she couldn't recall much about it.

Ramona crept down the stairs. The house was very quiet. She noticed that the rest of Michael's home matched her room nicely. Hand hewn and whittled furniture decorated each room. The living room held a roaring fire in a large fireplace on one wall, and the open area led into a snug kitchen and pantry. From there, Ramona could see a door that appeared to open out into a back yard. There were a few things that a woman's touch could add to the home, such as window dressings and rugs, but overall the house felt inviting and comfortable. She saw Mary, sitting by the fire, darning a pair of pants.

"Good morning."

"Good morning," replied Mary, standing to her feet and making her way into the kitchen.

"I'm so sorry, my dear, we would have waited for you to eat breakfast, but we weren't sure when you might want to get up. You had a long journey to recover from. The men have already eaten and gone to work, so we have the house to ourselves," said Mary, hurrying to get Ramona a plate.

"Of course, I wouldn't expect you to wait. I can't believe how late I slept. I was so tired, and that bedroom is really very comfortable."

"Michael made all the furniture himself. He's got quite the knack for it," said Mary, handing Ramona a plate piled high with eggs, and a slice of bread covered with butter and jam.

"Wow, he has a talent, that's for sure." Ramona walked to the table and sat down to eat. Mary sat across from her, the knitting still in her hands.

"Thank you. This is delicious." Ramona bit hungrily

into the bread. She was famished after so many days of travelling.

"You're most welcome. I'll show you around today, and when Michael and Fred come home from working on the new State Capitol tonight, maybe we can have dinner waiting for them. What do you say?"

"That sounds great," said Ramona, wondering how she was going to find her mother if she was going to be stuck in the house all day, every day, while Michael was at work.

I'll just have to find a way. Perhaps I can borrow the wagon. I'll have to earn his trust, so that he lets me take it out on my own. But how I wish I could just go to her now. Still, it is very cozy here, and they have all been so very welcoming. It won't be the worst thing to stay here a bit until I can get my bearings and figure out where Mother is.

When Michael and Fred came home from work that evening, he seemed to be in a pensive mood. Ramona watched him closely; he was even quieter than he had been the previous evening. Mary and Ramona bustled about the small kitchen, cooking fried bacon, cornbread and buttermilk for supper. Mary showed Ramona where everything was located while they worked, and the two of them chatted happily together.

Michael and Fred sat together by the fire, stoking it occasionally while Fred puffed on a pipe.

"How's the building coming along?" Mary called to them both, from the kitchen.

"Fine. It'll be another couple of years, they tell us," said Michael.

"Phew! That structure's going to be something, isn't it?"

"Sure is."

Ramona listened intently to the exchange, hoping to get some further insight into what Michael was like. The moment he'd walked in the door after work she had felt her pulse quicken. There was something about him that made her nervous, and she couldn't shake the feeling of wanting to be nearer to him. He had such a gentleness about him, and seemed to consider her feelings in everything he said and did. She could already see the warmth in his eyes when he looked at her.

Forget about Michael. I'm here to fetch Mother. I have to focus on finding out when he can take me to the university. After Mother and I return to New York I won't ever see him again, so there's no use in thinking about him. I need to just get him out of my head.

"Come and get it!" called Mary, breaking through Ramona's reverie. Ramona removed her apron and wiped her hands clean before carrying plates to the table.

The men made their way to the kitchen, Fred cleaning his pipe out first. As Michael took his seat, his arm brushed against Ramona's, sending a wave of tingles through her body. She started and looked up at him in surprise, wondering whether he had felt it too. His green eyes were staring at her quizzically, as though he were trying to read her thoughts.

"Excuse me, ma'am," he said politely as he removed his hat and sat down.

"Did you have a nice day?" asked Ramona. Her voice was uncharacteristically low.

"Thank you, I did. And you?"

The way he watched her made her squirm with pleasure. He seemed genuinely interested in what she had to say. Ramona nodded.

"Yes, thank you."

They barely spoke for the rest of the evening. Fred and Mary exchanged concerned glances. Fred shook his head at Mary, and she smiled pityingly at the two of them.

"There's chemistry there no doubt," she whispered to Fred, "but they're each too afraid to speak to the other. I guess that will change with time."

"It'd better," remarked Fred.

Chapter Nine

Michael

Michael had every intention of bringing up the topic of the wedding the following day. He'd lost his nerve the previous evening when his arm had brushed against Ramona's sending a jolt through his body. He'd felt as though his throat would close up entirely, but he was determined to find out where Ramona stood on the subject before work. When morning came and Ramona bounced down the stairs, looking glamorous and cosmopolitan, he lost his nerve once more and instead busied himself buttering a piece of bread.

This afternoon. After work. I'll speak with her then. It would be too hurried a conversation to have it now. No—afternoon is a much better time to talk.

When Michael got home from work that afternoon, Ramona wasn't there. Mary told him she'd taken a walk.

"By herself?" asked Michael.

"She insisted."

"But she doesn't know her way around."

Mary simply shook her head.

It wasn't long before Ramona returned, slipping off her hat and smoothing back her hair as she greeted him at the door. Once she had cleaned up and settled herself in the sitting room, Michael attempted to engage Ramona in conversation. But try as he might, she was constantly distracted, looking out the front window to the busy street beyond. It was as though she were searching for something, but for the life of him, Michael couldn't figure out what it could be.

When she wasn't distracted, she was chatty. Far chattier than any other woman Michael had ever met, and about a hundred times more talkative than he was. He didn't mind it so much in a way—he realized that if Ramona hadn't been so talkative and the conversation were left to him to spark there might well have been a constant silence between them. Generally he was glad that the pressure to carry a dialogue hadn't been left up to him. However, in this particular instance he was trying to get up the nerve and find an opportunity to broach the subject of the wedding.

He watched her as she chattered away, noticing the slope of her creamy neck beneath the thick curls of her dark hair. The way she bit her plump, red bottom lip, ever so gently, when she paused to consider her next statement. He felt perspiration forming on his forehead and his heart was racing. How would he ever get the words out?

The following evening Ramona was unusually quiet. Michael thought it might finally be his opportunity to speak with her privately. Mary and Fred were sitting together in the living room discussing an upcoming church picnic, and Ramona sat off to one side on her own. He cleared his throat and joined her by the front window, which was fast becoming her favorite place to sit.

"I like to watch what the people out there are up to," Ramona answered when he asked her why she liked the spot so much.

"Ramona…" Michael began, "are you, are you still happy with our…" He trailed off, clenching his jaw as he tried to force the words out, "arrangement? You're not disappointed in me, are you? I know sometimes these things can be awkward."

Ramona laughed a little, her cheeks flushing pink.

"Do you mean us getting married?"

"Well, yes. Actually, I was just wondering if you, when you might want to. Get married, that is."

Ramona raised one eyebrow, looking confused.

"I don't know. I hadn't really thought about it."

She hasn't thought about it? It's all I can think of. How can a woman travel across the country to marry a man, and when she arrives—not think about the wedding?

"What's going on, Ramona?"

Ramona's eyes flitted across the kitchen floorboards. Her discomfort was evident.

"Please," Michael said quietly. "Tell me the truth. Why are you really here?"

Ramona sighed, and pulled at a stray thread on her skirt, refusing to meet his gaze.

"I'm here to find my mother." Ramona turned her head back toward the window and stared off into the distance.

"Your mother?"

Ramona nodded. She kept watching people walking by the house through the window. Finally she met Michael's eyes with her own.

"Mother is here, somewhere in Austin. That's all I know."

"So that's why you came here? That's why you chose me?" He was barely able to shield the disappointment in his voice. It's all starting to make sense now. A woman as beautiful and glamorous as Ramona would never choose to marry a stranger in a pioneering town.

Michael spun on his heel and strode into the kitchen. Ramona rushed after him.

"I'm sorry," she said.

Michael heard the genuine distress in her voice.

"I never thought, oh, when the lady said I could be sent to Austin to marry a man, I guess I never really thought about the man on the other end. That he would be real. And sweet and kind like you are. I never had any intention of hurting you. I'm sorry if I have."

Michael lowered himself into a chair at the dining table, and Ramona slumped into a matching chair opposite him. She took a deep breath and told Michael the entire story. She started with her father's debts and the way he took his own life, and ended with her mother running away to Texas to marry a man Ramona had never met.

She leaned forward and gently placed a hand on Michael's arm. He stared down at it in astonishment, catching his breath at her touch.

"Michael, I'm sorry that I've used you. And most of all I'm sorry I wasn't honest with you from the start. I was just so desperate to find Mother. I wasn't thinking about anything else. Or anyone else."

She withdrew her hand and Michael felt he could breathe again.

"It's okay," he said gently. "I know what it's like to lose someone. I'm awful sorry for everything that's happened to you, Ramona. I had no idea. I don't judge you for what you've done. I want you to know that. But I will tell you that I'm disappointed."

Ramona managed a little smile. "You are such a kind man. I can't see why you would need to use a Mail Order Bride service in the first place! I'm sure women around here would be queuing up to marry you!"

Michael blushed and cleared his throat. "There aren't many woman around here like you, Ramona. I thought, well, I was still thinking actually, I know you're here to find your mother and all, but if you wanted I could still, I mean, we could still get married."

Ramona leaned back in her chair, away from him, and her face dropped.

"Never mind." Michael shook his head. "No, of course not. I'm sorry. It's all right, Ramona. Just forget the whole thing."

"Michael."

"It's fine." He managed to force a bright smile. "I'll help you find your mother and then you can go home."

Ramona looked at him quizzically. "Do you mean it, Michael?"

"Sure. I can help you find her. I know this town well. If your mother is in Austin, I'll be able to figure where she's at."

"You really are a kind man, Michael. Much kinder than I deserve."

Chapter Ten

Ramona

Ramona felt renewed when she woke up. Reaching for the window, she pushed her head through the opening and took a deep breath of the fresh morning air. The straw tick crunched pleasantly beneath her. She noticed that the flowers in the vase were now limp and turning brown.

I'll have to get fresh flowers from the garden. I'm sorry to think of leaving this pretty house. I was starting to believe coming here had been a mistake. I wasn't sure how long I could keep Michael from bringing up the subject of the wedding. But it has all worked out perfectly. He's so understanding. I thought he would put me back on the next train as soon as he found out why I was really here. I should have just told him the truth right from the beginning. He's so kind.

She leaned farther out the window and picked a cherry blossom from a nearby tree branch.

And Austin is such a nice town. Or, at least, it will be one day. It will be a shame to leave it, in a way.

She straightened up and shut the window. She was excited to get started looking for her mother. And now, she had help to do it, so there was no need to wait any longer.

Ramona bounded down the stairs. A fire cracked and spat in the hearth, and the smell of hot Johnnie cakes wafted up to greet her.

"Good morning all!"

"Good morning," came the reply from Michael, Mary and Fred as each looked up from the dining table where they were about to eat.

"So, Michael, when shall we start looking for Mother? I have a few ideas about where we might find her. She did leave me one clue. Do you remember I was asking you if you knew anybody at the university?"

Michael hid a smile behind his hand as Ramona sat down at the table. Clearing his throat he said, "Great. We can start after work today if you like? And yes, I do remember you asking that. We can start there if you like."

Ramona nodded quickly. "Yes, that would be perfect. I can't thank you enough."

"There's no need, really. I'm happy to help."

"You sure don't waste any time," said Fred, munching on fresh Johnnie cake smothered with butter and syrup.

"Sorry." Ramona blushed. "How are you all? Did you sleep well?"

Mary smiled. "Soundly, thank you, Ramona, and how about you?"

"Oh yes, I slept like a log. It's so comfortable in my bedroom, and the air coming through the window is so fresh, the birds sing prettily, and the scents wafting up from the gardens outside are just divine. Really, it is all very pleasant."

"I'm glad you like it." Michael smiled at her shyly.

"It's perfect," said Ramona, taking a bite of the golden cake on her plate.

"Well, we've got to get going." Fred stood to his feet, and leaned forward to kiss Mary on the cheek. "We'll see you ladies this evening."

"Oh dear, let me make some lunch for you, I'm afraid I overslept again. You're going to think I'm such a layabout, but honestly I've never had to take care of anyone other than myself before," cried Ramona, jumping to her feet.

"No mind, I'm not used to having someone take care of me at that." Michael's face flushed red.

She hurried to the kitchen, and made sandwiches for the two men with cured ham and mustard on thick slices of freshly baked bread. Taking their lunch pails from beneath the counter, she filled them with apples and oatmeal cookies that she and Mary had baked the previous day. Covering the pails with a cloth which she tied in place, she reached for their water cups that were drying on the sink, and handed the pails and cups to the men.

"There. Now you'll not go hungry."

"Thank you, Ramona." Fred nodded his head at her, then turned to leave.

"Thank you." Michael took the pail and cup, and stood in front of her as though he were about to say something, but couldn't get the words out. Then he simply said, "Bye," and ducked his head.

Ramona smiled and returned to the table to eat her breakfast. Michael threw her one last glance, then hurried out the front door after Fred, carrying his lunch pail in one hand and his water cup in the other, his black hat pushed firmly down on his head against the wind.

"Bye!" Ramona shouted at his retreating back. He waved without turning around, as he scurried down the road.

Ramona climbed up into the wagon holding lightly to Michael's hand and toting a small basket under one arm. It was still light out, but they wouldn't have long to search before twilight descended.

"What's in the basket?" asked Michael, steadying her and guiding her to her seat on the wagon bench.

"I've packed us a picnic dinner."

Michael eyed the package hungrily. He leapt up beside her and took the reins in his hands. He hadn't had a chance to eat anything since he'd finished work. Instead he had rushed home and harnessed Sadie in the wagon to take Ramona out searching for her mother as quickly as he could in order to make the most of the daylight.

"Thank you, Ramona. We'll be able to stop and enjoy that in a little while."

He guided the horse out onto the street, her hooves clip-clopping on the dusty road. "So you really have no idea where she might be?"

Ramona shook her head. "Other than that she came here to marry someone who works at the university? No. He's a professor, I believe. His name is Art Franklin."

Michael raised his eyebrows. "Well, at least that's something to go on."

Ramona nodded.

"It's a start. And better than nothing. I don't care if

I have to walk down every street in Austin and knock on every last door. I'll find her."

Michael looked at Ramona, impressed.

"I have to say, I do admire your courage. To come out here from New York with very little idea as to where you mother is or if you'll find her. Most people wouldn't even try. They'd give up. But you're so positive, and determined."

He grinned at her, and pushed his black hat back on his head.

"I always like to see the bright side of the situation. I try to find the positives where I can."

Michael clucked to the horse, and she picked up her pace.

"I noticed that about you." He chuckled. "Well, we've got an uphill battle ahead of us! But I'm sure we can manage it. We'll find her, it's just a matter of time."

They spent the next two weeks looking for Ramona's mother every day after Michael finished his long shifts at the construction site. They started with the roads and streets near the university, thinking that someone there might know Ramona's mother or some piece of information about her whereabouts. So far, no one they had spoken to knew anything about a history professor called Art Franklin, or his new wife.

"Don't give up," Michael told her.

"I won't."

But Ramona was quickly losing hope. Surely, if they lived nearby someone would recognize their names? Maybe they hadn't stayed long and had already moved on to a new town. She tried to hide her diminishing faith from Michael. He, in turn, kept encouraging her to pray about it. So she did. She asked God for guidance. She begged Him for strength. She prayed fervently for wisdom to know what to do should she never find her mother. Michael was always there, by her side, comforting her when she was turned away yet again by another passerby who knew nothing of Professor Franklin.

"You've just got to keep trying," Michael said one day when he could tell that Ramona's spirits were low. "How about I finish work a little early this evening, so we've got the extra time to look. I have a good feeling about tonight. I think we'll finally find her."

"Okay." Ramona nodded. "Let's try again," she said, forcing a smile onto her face.

The wind brought a change in the air that evening. Ramona could feel the temperature dropping with the breeze that blew in off the desert, carrying with it a thick layer of red dust covering everything in its path. They headed out as usual, Ramona carrying their picnic basket under her arm. They rode to the university in the wagon, the silence of the evening broken only by the early call of a screech owl gliding between the trees overhead. They found a new neighborhood they hadn't canvassed yet, and climbed out of the wagon to investigate by foot.

Michael had to hurry to keep up with Ramona's stride, which had turned into a nervous skip as she danced across the dirt road.

What happens when I do find Mother? I'll be leaving here and going back to New York. Isn't that what I want? Then, why does the thought of it make me feel so wretched? The fact is, I don't know if I want to leave Austin. Or Michael.

The truth hit her like a slap across the cheek.

I don't want to leave him. But how do I tell him that? He's accepted that we're not getting married. He seems fine with it, as if he's relieved by not having to go through with it after all. Oh, what a mess I've made for myself. I should never have come here.

"What's wrong, Ramona?" Michael's voice pierced through her thoughts.

"Nothing." Ramona pulled her shawl around her tightly. "I just want to get home quickly tonight."

Michael looked pleased. "Well, let's hurry up then," he said, quickening his own pace to match hers. They walked side by side. Michael glanced at Ramona, a curious look on his face. She smiled at him, and felt the glow of a nervous flush creeping up her neck and onto her cheeks.

The stillness of the cool evening was pierced by a sudden "BANG." People ran in every direction, ducking for cover as Ramona realized a pistol had been shot. She could hear shouting, and then two more popping sounds, as bullets flew through the air around them.

There was chaos in the street now. Ramona instinctively jumped to where she thought Michael was standing. "Michael?" she called out. She heard the sound of heavy hooves pounding on the road beneath her feet. The sound grew louder. She spun around. There, thundering toward her was a white stallion with wild eyes. The beast whinnied and kicked up dust with its hind legs as it ran. A black wagon tethered behind it was bouncing up and down looking as though it might break free at any moment.

There was no time for Ramona to get out of the creature's path. It was barreling toward her so quickly that she barely had time to think of what to do. She went to leap out of the way, but the next thing Ramona knew, her head hit something hard, and the entire world went black.

"Michael," Ramona murmured, looking up into his kind, green eyes. His arms felt so soft, so comforting, and she pressed herself into him, her head dizzy from more than the wound.

I could stay here forever.

Ramona lay still in Michael's warm embrace.

"I don't know what happened. There was a gunshot, and a horse. I couldn't get out of the way."

"Shhh," he said, almost laughing in his relief that she was okay. "Try not to speak. Try not to move. I'm going to get you home."

Once they were home, the injury was all but forgotten. Ramona sat up in bed, bright-eyed and talkative. Michael brought her a bowl of steaming hot soup and gently suggested she ought to get some rest. She agreed to sleep for a while after she'd eaten and Mary bustled about the room, plumping her pillows, and fluffing her sheets. She opened the window, then closed it again, undecided on which would be best.

"I'm fine," said Ramona. "Really, Mary, I'm okay. Just a bit shaken up, that's all. I'll have a little sleep, and I'll be as good as new, I promise."

Mary stroked Ramona's forehead once, pushing a few stray hairs from her face. She smiled, then turned to leave the room.

"You call me if you need anything," she said, concern written clearly across her pretty face.

"I will. I'm fine."

Michael checked in on her after an hour, and handed her another cup of soup as she sat up to slowly sip the steaming broth. "You know, Ramona, I was so worried about you today. I thought that, I thought you'd been hurt real bad."

Michael's eyes searched hers, as if to look for some kind of sign. Not finding what he was looking for, he sighed and got to his feet.

Ramona wondered what she had done to cause him to leave so suddenly.

"Good night, Ramona. I hope you are feeling better in the morning."

She smiled up at him. "Good night, Michael."

Ramona sat up in bed for a while, staring at the closed door. She tried to tell herself that she was feeling low because another day had passed and she was still no closer to finding her mother. She lay back against the pillow, her dark hair fanning out across it. Deep down, she knew the truth. As soon as their mission was over, as soon as they found her mother, then she would have no reason to stay in Austin. She'd have no reason to stay with Michael. She'd be returning to New York and would never lay eyes on him again. The thought made her jolt upright in bed.

Ramona sighed and lay back against her pillow again, reaching a hand to pull back the lace curtain. Outside she could see a clear star-filled sky.

For so long I've chased my dreams, and they've always seemed so far out of reach. As far away as those stars. But what if my dreams—my happiness—could be found elsewhere? Could I be content to live in a small dusty town? Is it possible that Michael still wants me?

* * *

Michael closed the door to Ramona's room softly behind him and leaned back against it, his eyes closed. When Ramona had been trampled by the stallion, he was sure she had been killed.

He'd run to her, and held her limp body in his arms. The pain that had filled his gut in that moment made him realize how deep his feelings for her ran.

I've got to do something to tempt her to stay here. With me. I've got to find a way to tell her how I feel. If she doesn't feel the same way, at least I will have been honest with her. I can't do more than that.

Chapter Eleven

Michael

Even though Ramona seemed to be losing interest in their search for her mother, Michael grew more determined with each passing day to find her. He had gotten the idea into his head, that if he could just do this for her, if he could reunite her with her mother, that she would see him for who he was. That maybe she'd see him as the kind of man she might want to marry.

Every evening while they searched, Michael was attentive to her every need. He carried her through any muddy patches on the ground. He always found her a place to sit when she was tired. He told her stories as they rode in the wagon, and guided her gently through the rough streets of Austin. Every day Michael fell harder and harder for Ramona.

If only Ramona could see what I see. We could be so good together. I wish she'd give me a chance to prove that.

Each day Ramona seemed to let down another wall, opening herself up to Michael, and drawing him in at the same time. She told him about the heartache and ostracism she and her mother had endured after her father's suicide. She spoke about their poverty and her mother's fight to find a steady job.

"Sometimes we would have one meal between us. That would have to last us three or four days," she said, as they rested in a park in the center of town. "Even so, Mother never made me give up on my dreams, she always supported me."

"I'm sorry, Ramona. That must have been hard on you." Michael was quiet for a moment. "And you still want to find your Ma, don't you? It just seems to me like you've almost given up lately."

Ramona nodded as she bit her bottom lip. "I know now that she most likely doesn't want to be found, I can't give up hope just yet. My friend Elizabeth was right. I don't think she'll want to come back to New York with me. But I want to find her anyhow. To tell her, to tell her that I love her no matter what."

Back to New York.

Those words pierced through Michael's heart. He dropped his head and looked at the green grass beneath him. She has no intention of staying here, no matter the outcome. Tony was right.

Michael felt stunned as the full weight of her words hit him. The disappointment crushed his chest and he sucked in a deep breath.

I've been fooling myself. I should have known it from the start. Ramona came here with a mission. And it never included marrying me.

"I just wanted to tell you, Michael, that I'm so grateful you haven't given up on me or on Mother yet."

"Of course." He stared at the ground.

"I see how hard you work, how many hours you put in during the day on the construction site. And then, on top of all that, you take me out searching for Mother after hours." Ramona's voice began to break a little. "I don't even know how to thank you, Michael. Gosh, in all my life, no one has shown me the kindness that you have."

Michael heard the emotion in her voice and he looked up, startled. "Ramona, please, what is the matter?"

Ramona collapsed in tears. "I just feel like we are never going to find her! Oh it all seems so hopeless! And I feel so badly that I have dragged you into this fruitless search."

"Shhh." Michael reached over and placed his arm around her shoulder, pulling her into him as she wept. "Please don't give up. I haven't."

Michael hadn't given up hope that they would find Maria. But he had given up hope that Ramona would ever want to marry him.

"What did I tell ya?" Tony said the following day as he drove his shovel into the dirt. "I warned ya, Michael."

"I know," he said quietly. "You were right. I'll help Ramona find her mother. Then I'll drive her back to the stagecoach and move on with my life. I won't try for another Mail Order Bride after this, Tony. That ought to make you happy."

Tony's face grew a little red. "I'm sorry, Michael. I don't mean to take pleasure from your situation." He stopped digging. "Though I must say I'm surprised you are still going to help her." Tony let out a sigh. "You're a good man, Michael. Perhaps I ought to tell you something. I've been holding onto it in the hopes that Ramona might come around after all and fall for you—heck you're the best man I know. She's a fool not to see it."

Michael stood up straight. "What's that, Tony?"

Tony's face had flushed a deep red.

"I think I know where Ramona's mother is."

"What?" Michael threw his shovel down. "What are you talking about?"

Tony lifted his hands up. "Hey, I don't know for sure. But, the Italians in town, they tend to stick together. Gossip about each other, you know. Anyway, I heard about this Italian woman who moved here from New York. Married some snooty Professor or something."

Michael's face was dark as thunder. "Tony, why did you keep this from me?"

Tony looked at the ground and shrugged. "Like I said, I was tryin' to help you. I thought that if she spent a bit more time with you, she'd fall hard. I'm sorry."

Michael shook his head. But she is leaving, no matter what. He walked over to his friend and growled, fiercely. "Tony, you tell me where she is! Right now!"

"Here," said Tony, handing the letter to Michael the following day. The sky was threatening and black with skidding clouds. The air about them was heavy, and they both had sweat dripping down the sides of their faces and soaking their shirts. Tony avoided eye contact with Michael, looking everywhere else but his face. Just then, the heavens opened up and fat drops of cold rain pelted down on them, causing the ground beneath their feet to become muddy and slippery within moments.

"I don't know if you're going to like what's in there."

"What are you talking about, Tony?" Michael didn't seem to notice the rain.

Tony shoved his hands in his pockets. "My Mama," he whispered. "She knew Maria. Sort of. They ran in the same circles. They weren't close. She got this letter from her husband."

Michael looked at him, his eyes narrowing. "What do you mean, she 'knew' Maria? What happened to her? Where is she now?"

"Just read the letter, Michael."

Michael unfolded the sheet of paper in his hands. His eyes scanned over the contents. He quickly re-folded it and closed his eyes, shaking his head.

"I can't tell Ramona this. And you can't breathe a word of it to her either. You got me? You owe me that much at least!"

Tony nodded. He lifted his head, his eyes meeting Michael's. "I promise."

Chapter Twelve

Ramona

Michael avoided Ramona all that evening. He came home from work late, and ate his supper in silence.

"Are we going out tonight?" she asked eagerly.

"No. It's raining out."

"Oh."

I've pushed him too hard. Taken his patience and good nature for granted. Of course he's tired of searching. Tired of helping me. He probably just wants me to leave, so he can get back to his life.

Ramona retreated into herself and sat quietly on a whittled wooden chair, knitting. She wondered what she could do, if anything, to get back into Michael's good graces. She'd made him supper and a pudding for dessert, but he didn't even acknowledge her effort. Mary and Fred seemed to sense the tension between the two of them, and had disappeared to their room directly after the meal. After cleaning up in the kitchen and knitting for as long as she could stand to, Ramona spent the rest of the evening tiptoeing around and staying out of Michael's way.

What can I do to show him that I appreciate everything he has done for me?

Ramona looked around and saw Michael's muddy work clothes. I know—I'll scrub his boots and clean his trousers and jacket then lay them by the fire to dry. Michael will be surprised when he wakes up tomorrow morning.

It wasn't long before Michael excused himself for bed, striding out of the room with a scowl on his handsome face. Ramona hastily grabbed his work clothes from the floor where he had left them by the door. Before she put the coat through the ringer she made sure the pockets were empty.

That's when the note drifted to the floor.

Ramona saw only one thing as she picked up the letter. The signature on the bottom that read, "Art Franklin."

"Ramona, what are you doing?" Michael raced into the room and grabbed the coat from her grasp. Too late, he saw the letter in her trembling hands.

"Ramona, please."

"You know where my mother is?" Ramona's eyes flashed as she waved the letter in front of his face. "And you kept it from me? For how long, Michael?"

She took a step backward, moving away from him, her curls swirling about her shoulders.

"How could you do this to me? You know how tormented I've been about it all." Her voice broke and she sobbed loudly. She stopped, and her eyes widened. "Did you keep this from me because you wanted me to stay? Or do you just not care about me at all?"

"Ramona, it's not like that."

Michael lifted his hands toward her, reaching for her. But Ramona backed further away.

"Did you think if you just kept lying to me and hid Mother's location from me that I would stay here with you forever? Did you think that I would give up and marry you? Or were you trying to punish me for hurting you?"

"Ramona please, let me explain. I only got that letter today. Please, you have to believe me."

Ramona studied Michael's face, looking for a sign that he was telling the truth. "I don't know what to believe. How can I trust you?"

She pressed the letter to her chest, and headed for the door. "Maybe I'm just too naive. Here I was trying to think of ways to repay you for all of your kindnesses to me. I never thought you would stoop to something like this."

Ramona opened the front door and rushed through it into the stormy night.

Michael ran after her, grabbing her by the arm, the falling rain soaking them both to the bone. "Ramona! Where are you going?"

She tried to shake off his grasp, waving the letter at him. "I'm going to find Art Franklin, and don't try to stop me!"

"Ramona, you can't."

"Of course I can! You've kept this from me long enough! I'm going right now!" Ramona tried to wriggle free of Michael's grip on her arm, but he held on too tightly.

"Let me go, Michael! You're hurting me!"

He dropped her arm, both his own hanging helplessly

by his sides. The rain ran in rivulets down his face, and his eyes, filled with sadness, found Ramona's.

"Ramona, your mother—she passed away."

Ramona stopped struggling. All the color drained from her face. Her lips were turning blue from the cold, and her teeth chattered silently. She staggered toward him, and he caught her by one arm.

"No," Ramona whispered with a shake of her head. "You're lying again." Her voice was hoarse. "You just, you're just trying to keep me from finding her!"

Michael's face fell. "Ramona, do you really think I would lie about something like that? Don't you know me at all?"

Ramona dropped to her knees, overcome with emotion.

Michael crouched down beside her, and pulled her into his arms but she pushed him away. Then, she fell in a heap on the muddy ground, her sobs muffled by the thunder of the downpour. Michael pulled her close to him again, lifting her cheek and placing it against his chest. This time she didn't resist, and nestled in closer still. He laced one hand through her thick hair and rubbed her back gently with the other. Overwhelmed and dazed by the news, Ramona wondered where she would go. She had nothing and no one. She didn't even have the money to return home. She'd never see her mother again. What would she do?

Chapter Thirteen

Ramona

"You don't have to do this, you know," Michael said gently.

Ramona took a bold step forward and knocked on Art Franklin's front door.

God, give me strength.

"I have to," she whispered. "I need to hear it for myself. I need to know what happened to Mother."

Michael nodded. "I understand. I'm here with you, if you need me," Michael whispered.

Ramona nodded. Her hands were laced in front of her as she waited for Mr. Franklin to answer the door. She was expecting a kind man, much like her father had been. Someone warm and sincere, who would have taken care of her mother during her last days.

"Yes?"

The door opened, and a man with thinning hair and a stern face stood on the threshold. He seemed aggravated by their presence, tapping the doorframe with his fingers as though it might hurry them along.

"Hello. My name is Ramona Selmer. And this is a friend of mine, Michael Newhill. My mother was Maria Selmer—I believe you knew her."

"Oh my!" he peered down at Ramona through squinting eyes. "Well, well. I was married to Maria, yes, but she certainly never mentioned a daughter."

"Never?"

"No, not once. I assure you. And you are here because?"

"Well, I heard that she died. And I want to find out what happened." Ramona's voice trembled as she spoke, and she took a deep breath in an attempt to calm herself.

Art sighed. "Would you like some tea?" he asked in a way that made Ramona feel as though the correct answer would be 'no.'

She nodded her head and followed Art into his sitting room. Michael trailed along behind them. Ramona shot a look at him over her shoulder. She could tell from Michael's face that he felt uncomfortable in Art's home with the rows of bookshelves and store-bought furnishings.

I'm so glad he's here with me. I don't know if I could bear it alone.

Art fetched a tray with a kettle full of steaming tea and teacups. He served them each a cup of tea, then he grabbed a pipe from a side table, and packed it with tobacco before seating himself on a stuffed brown corduroy chair. Ramona settled into a sunken chair with green and gold upholstery, and Michael stood uncomfortably by the window, looking out onto the street beyond. Art peered down his thin nose at Ramona as he spoke, the freshly packed pipe hanging from between his lips.

"Scarlet fever," he said simply. "I'm afraid it was nothing more glamorous than that." He cast a disapproving look at Ramona as he spoke. "It took hold of her quickly." Art stood, and banged the contents of the pipe out onto an ashtray, shaking his head slowly. "Barely worth even getting married. Although I suppose she was desperate. Especially after what that coward of a man did to her."

Ramona opened her mouth to speak but only a squeak came out. She had to clear her throat and try again.

"And did she—did she leave me anything?"

Ramona sat very still as she waited for the answer.

Art rolled his eyes. "I was wondering when that would come up. Looking for money are you?" He shot Ramona a look of disgust. "No. Nothing. She came here with nothing and she left this world with nothing." His eyebrows shot up. "I suggest you go back to New York. There's naught here for you."

Ramona's lips began to tremble. Michael was staring at her in distress. "Ramona, let's just go."

She stood to her feet and approached Art, who was leaning against the mantle with the empty pipe dangling from his bottom lip.

"I'm not here for your money. I just wanted to know if she left me anything of sentimental value. If only she'd stayed with me, she should never have married you—you didn't deserve her!" She held her voice steady as she stepped toward Art, her eyes never leaving his. "My father was a kind man, who got himself into some awful trouble. And my mother was a beautiful woman. You should be pleased to have been married to her no matter for how long! And she didn't leave this world with nothing. I loved her, and that is something!"

Art stepped back, stumbling over a poker beside the fireplace, as Ramona inched forward. But she was finished. She had nothing more to say.

"Ramona was only here to find out what happened to her mother," Michael said, with a fierceness that Ramona hadn't heard before. "She wasn't looking for money. Especially not from you." He reached for Ramona's arm, tucking it gently under his own. "Come on, let's get out of here."

Outside, the very last of Ramona's courage dissolved. She made it around the corner before she collapsed.

"That man!" she said, as Michael reached out to hold her up. "He was horrible! Oh, how could Mother ever have married him? I bore it for so long because I truly believed she had found happiness, and I so wanted her to be happy. But how could she have been happy with him?"

Ramona wept and shook her head. "At least I know now." She looked up at Michael glumly. "Though I feel rather naive. All this time, expecting the best, trying to remain positive. What good did that do me?" She turned and looked over her shoulder in the direction of Art Franklin's house. "There was no happy ending here."

"There was nothing you could have done," Michael said gently. "You did the best you could, given the situation."

Ramona nodded. "Well, things certainly seem hopeless now. Art was right about one thing: I should go home. I have nothing. No one, no family in this whole world. I'm on my own, and it's time I figured out what to do with my life now."

Michael looked hurt. “No one?”

Ramona shook her head as she sadly turned away. “No one. Let’s go—I ought to go back to your place and pack.”

Chapter Fourteen

Michael stared at the purple satin bag with the green bow. It seemed to him like it was only yesterday that he'd first carried that bag to his wagon. Now he was about to take it back to the stagecoach.

Ramona stepped forward. "How do I look?" she asked. She spun around in her long purple and white calico dress, her hair cascading over her shoulders.

"You look real nice." Michael gave her a sad smile.

He could have sworn that the smile Ramona returned had the same tinge of sadness to it. But she brightened as she said, "At least I will be back in time to audition for Broadway again. And thank you—" she placed her gloved hand on Michael's arm "—thank you for lending me the money for my ticket. I will pay you back by wire transfer as soon as I possibly can. I promise."

Michael nodded. "There's no need, Ramona, it was a gift."

He reached for the suitcase but stopped before he picked it up. "Hey," he said, glancing at the grandfather clock in the hallway. "We still have time before the coach is due to arrive." He smiled at her. "We never did go on that picnic. I didn't get a chance to show you the university properly. We were always in a rush."

Michael caught the look on Ramona's face at the mention of the university. "Sorry," he said hurriedly. "Of course you don't want to go there. Not after everything that has happened."

Ramona shook her head slowly. "No, I don't mind," she murmured. "In fact, I would love to go. I won't let Art Franklin ruin our last day together. Let's pack a picnic and go."

"You know, it really is beautiful here," Ramona commented, as they settled down on a picnic blanket in the university gardens. White and pink flowers surrounded them and the grass beneath them was fresh and soft. Michael's presence beside her made her stomach flutter.

"Yes, the university is lovely," Michael commented, reaching out for a sandwich, his eyes never leaving her face.

"Not just the university. I mean Austin," Ramona said wistfully. "I almost wish." She dropped her head, afraid to say what she wanted to.

Michael cleared his throat. "I'm sure New York has far more going for it than this little town."

"Yes. I suppose so."

Ramona looked away.

He wants me to go. This is just his way of saying goodbye. She looked around at the pretty garden with the flowers swaying gently in the fall breeze. I shouldn't read any more into it than that.

"If you were to stay here, for some reason, Austin has a theater you know. A pretty decent one, I think. You'd have a good chance of getting into one of the shows there. It's not Broadway, but it's something."

Ramona listened intently as she took in her surroundings, soaking in the peacefulness of the park, the beauty of the flowers, and the emptiness of the clear sky. She looked back at Michael. "No matter what happens in the future, Michael, please know how much I appreciate everything you have done for me. I have truly cherished my time here. Never in my life has anyone shown me such kindness. Never in my life have I felt like someone..." Ramona's throat closed up.

Loved me so much, she wanted to say.

But can it be true? Can he truly love me? Or is he just a good man? Kindness comes so naturally to him that I oughtn't to take his actions toward me personally. He no doubt would have treated anyone the same way.

Michael stood up. He seemed flustered.

"Let's take a walk down by the fountain," he said quietly, reaching for Ramona's hand to pull her up.

They crossed a bridge that stood over a small lake with a fountain in the center of it. Michael paused in the center and leaned over the side, watching the ducks sail by beneath them. "You know, I helped to build this bridge," he said softly.

"I didn't know that," Ramona said, surprised.

Michael nodded. "Years ago now. This site was one of my first jobs, when I was just fifteen."

"You went to work young," Ramona said, surprised.

"My parents believe that hard work makes a man strong." He stood still and stared at the tall buildings surrounding them.

"I would have liked to have gone to university, you know." Michael smiled ruefully. "I know it was impossible, but still."

"I'm sure you would have done very well," Ramona whispered. She impulsively reached up and tipped Michael's face toward hers. "You're a good man. You work hard. And you're so kind and patient, and, well, you're everything good."

Michael stood looking at her, his eyes darkened with emotion. He was so close to her, she could smell him, and could hear his shallow breathing. Without thinking, Ramona stood up on her tiptoes and pressed her lips against Michael's. She felt the unexpected softness of his lips on her own, and a shiver of pleasure ran through her body.

Ramona saw the look of shock on Michael's face as she pulled away.

Oh, why did I do that?

Ramona was mortified. She brought her hands up to her face to hide her blushing cheeks.

"I'm sorry. I'm sorry, Michael."

Ramona spun on her heel and ran through the university grounds, clutching her hands to her breast.

"Ramona, wait."

Michael chased after her, running quickly behind her until he caught her by the arm.

"Wait! Don't leave, please."

"Oh Michael, I'm so embarrassed," she whispered.

"What must you think of me? A lady doesn't do something like that."

But Ramona's embarrassment faded as she stared up into Michael's piercing green eyes. He smiled at her and pulled her close.

"What do I think? I think you're the most wonderful, courageous, beautiful woman I've ever met. That's what I think of you."

Ramona's face broke into a smile as she let out a ringing laugh, her eyes filling with tears at the same time. "You do?"

"I do," Michael whispered. This time it was he who took the lead. Michael wrapped his arms around Ramona and lifted her so that their lips could press together again. This time the kiss seemed to last forever, and Ramona wished that it would. It was Michael who finally broke them apart. He whispered into her ear, "And I have been wanting to kiss you like that since the first moment I saw you all covered in dust and dirt in the street."

Ramona laughed again, and wiped the happy tears from her eyes with her gloved fingers. Michael dropped to his knees in the green grass. Holding her hands in his, he gazed up into her eyes, a tender grin spreading across his face.

"Ramona, will you stay here in Austin and marry me?"

He seemed to hold his breath as he waited for her answer.

"Of course I will, Michael. I can't imagine my life without you now. You've ruined me for anything or anyone else."

"I love you, Ramona."

"I love you too, Michael," Ramona whispered, as they kissed again, this time, neither of them breaking the embrace.

* * * * *

SPECIAL EXCERPT FROM

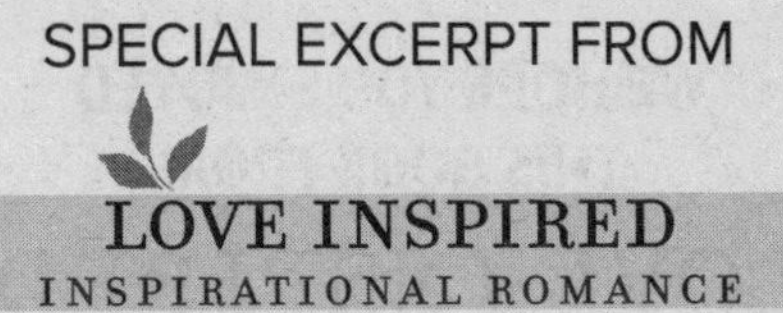

When a television reporter must go into hiding, she finds a haven deep in Amish country. Could she fall in love with the simple life—and a certain Amish man?

Read on for a sneak preview of The Amish Newcomer *by Patrice Lewis.*

"Isaac, we have a visitor. This is Leah Porte. She's an *Englischer* friend of ours, staying with us a few months. Leah, this is Isaac Sommer."

For a moment Isaac was struck dumb by the newcomer. With her dark hair tamed back under a *kapp*, and her chocolate eyes, he barely noticed the ugly red scar bisecting her right cheek.

Leah stepped forward. "How do you do?"

"Fine, *danke*. Where do you come from?"

"California."

"Please, sit. Both of you." Edith Byler gestured toward the table.

Isaac found himself opposite Leah and gazed at her as the family gathered around the table. When all heads bowed in silence, he found himself praying he could get to know the visitor better.

At once, chatter broke out as the family reached for food.

"We hope you'll have a pleasant stay with us." Ivan Byler scooped corn onto his plate .

"I…I'm not familiar with your day-to-day life." The woman toyed with her fork. "I don't want to be seen as a freeloader."

"What is it you did before you came here?" Ivan asked.

"I was a television journalist," she replied. Isaac saw her touch her wounded cheek and glance toward him. "But after my…my car accident, I couldn't do my job anymore."

LIEXP0820

Journalist! What kind of God-sent coincidence was that? He smiled. “Maybe I should have you write some articles for my magazine.”

“Magazine?”

Edith explained, “Isaac started a magazine for Plain people. He uses a computer to create it. The bishop gave him permission.”

“An Amish man using a computer?”

“Many *Englischers* have misconceptions of how much technology the *Leit* allows,” Ivan intervened. “You won’t find computers in our homes, or cell phones. But while we try to live not *of* the world, we still live *in* the world, and sometimes technology is needed to keep our businesses running. So, some bishops have decided a little technology is allowed.”

“What’s the magazine about?” Leah asked.

“Whatever appeals to Plain people. Farming. Businesses. Land management.”

“And you want *me* to write for it?” she asked. “I don’t know anything about those topics.”

“But that’s what a journalist does, ain’t so? Learn about new topics,” Isaac replied. Her opposition made him more determined. “Besides, you’re about to get a crash course while you stay here. Maybe you’ll learn something.”

“I already said I had no intention of being a freeloader.”

He nodded. “*Gut.* Then prove it. You can write me an article about what you learn.”

“Sure,” she snapped. “How hard could it be?”

He grinned. “You’ll find out soon enough.”

SPECIAL EXCERPT FROM

HARLEQUIN

SPECIAL EDITION

Real estate developer Brittany Doyle is eager to bring the mountain town of Gallant Lake into the twenty-first century...by changing everything. Hardware store owner Nate Thomas hates change. These opposites refuse to compromise, except when it comes to falling in love.

Read on for a sneak peek at
Changing His Plans,
the next book in the Gallant Lake Stories miniseries by Jo McNally.

He stuck his head around the corner of the fasteners aisle just in time to see a tall brunette stagger into the revolving seed display. Some of the packets went flying, but she managed to steady the display before the whole thing toppled. He took in what probably had been a very nice silk blouse and tailored trouser suit before she was drenched in the storm raging outside. The heel on one of the ridiculously high heels she was wearing had snapped off, explaining why she was stumbling around.

"Having a bad morning?"

The woman looked up in annoyance, strands of dark, wet hair falling across her face.

"You could say that. I don't suppose you have a shoe repair place in this town?" She looked at the bright red heel in her hand.

Nate shook his head as he approached her. "Nope. But hand it over. I'll see what I can do."

A perfectly shaped brow arched high. "Why? Are you going to cobble them back together with—" she gestured around widely "—maybe some staples or screws?"

"Technically, what you just described is the definition of cobbling, so yeah. I've got some glue that'll do the trick." He met her gaze calmly. "It'd be a lot easier to do if you'd take the shoe off. Unless you also think I'm a blacksmith?"

He was teasing her. Something about this soaking-wet woman still having so much…regal bearing…amused Nate. He wasn't usually a fan of the pearl-clutching country club set who strutted through Gallant Lake on the weekends and referred to his family's hardware store as "adorable." But he couldn't help admiring this woman's ability to hold on to her superiority while looking like she accidentally went to a water park instead of the business meeting she was dressed for. To be honest, he also admired the figure that expensive red suit was clinging to as it dripped water on his floor.

He held out his hand. "I'm Nate Thomas. This is my store."

She let out an irritated sigh. "Brittany Doyle." She slid her long, slender hand into his and gripped with surprising strength. He held it for just a half second longer than necessary before shaking off the odd current of interest she invoked in him.

HSEEXP0820